GW00726693

Whip Smart

A Salt Mine Novel

Joseph Browning   Suzi Yee

Text Copyright © 2020 by Joseph Browning and Suzi Yee

Published by Expeditious Retreat Press
Cover by J Caleb Design
Edited by Elizabeth VanZwoll

For information regarding Joseph Browning and Suzi Yee's novels and to subscribe to their mailing list, see their website at https://www.joseph-browning.com

To follow them on Twitter: https://twitter.com/Joseph_Browning

To follow Joseph on Facebook: https://www.facebook.com/joseph.browning.52

To follow Suzi on Facebook: https://www.facebook.com/SuziYeeAuthor/

To follow them on MeWee: https://mewe.com/i/josephbrowning

By Joseph Browning and Suzi Yee

THE SALT MINE NOVELS
Money Hungry
Feeding Frenzy
Ground Rules
Mirror Mirror
Bottom Line
Whip Smart
Rest Assured
Hen Pecked
Brain Drain

Chapter One

Detroit, Michigan, USA
22nd of September, 10:00 p.m. (GMT-4)

The hard rain drummed against the windows, forming rivulets along the panes of glass. A flash of lightning streaked through the sky, and Sarah held the warm mug of cocoa in both hands as she started counting. *One...two...three... four...five...* the crack of thunder erupted before she could reach six. The residual low rumbles in the distant night sky confirmed her count—the storm was in retreat. She loved a good thunderstorm, especially when she was safely indoors to appreciate it...although there was something to be said about playing in the rain.

The summer had been long and hot, and it wasn't quite ready to relent, but it was fighting a losing battle. All the signs were there: the shortening days, the dropping temperatures, and the precipitous dips in barometric pressure that were coming more frequently. The transition from berry bounty to apple harvesting had already begun and soon, it would be time for Sarah to pick out a pumpkin straight from the patch. The rally cry had already been raised against the evils of pumpkin spice, not that it slowed popularity or consumption. No, resist as it may, summer would yield eventually and its surrender would usher in a new season.

Sarah always loved autumn, which she loosely defined as anything that required a light jacket or a sweater, not the puffy winter coat that hung in the back of her closet. It wasn't just the joy of getting warm and cozy against the chill or the cold-induced carb-loading; autumn heralded the holiday season, starting off with Halloween.

She turned her attention back to the notebook in her lap and considered the sketches and doodles. It wasn't too late to produce a killer costume, but she knew she only had so many nights and weekends left to spare. By this time last year, she had already started sewing. As of late, however, she'd had more important undertakings.

Sarah ran her hand through her short hair and reflexively stroked the red jade charm on the choker around her neck. Her fingers traced its smooth familiar contours. There were all sorts of powers attributed to the precious stone for those who believed in that sort of thing—a talisman of good luck, a channel for power and vitality, a stimulator of life force, nothing short of a warrior's stone. Not that Sarah subscribed to such notions; she only knew what called to her.

The rap of a tree limb on the window quickened as the wind picked up outside, bringing her back to the here and now. The pensive brunette finished the last of her hot cocoa and removed the cold pack from her right thigh to assess the damage. A fist-sized collage of blacks, blues, and angry reds glared at her. It was tender to the touch despite the general numbness from the icing, but it was nothing a few ibuprofen and time wouldn't mend. She'd weathered worse and knew this was far from the last bruise she'd have.

Sarah gingerly rose from the couch, unlocking the joints that had stiffened in place during her respite. After a few steps, her body remembered how to walk again and she returned the reusable pack to the freezer—it would be responsible for keeping tomorrow's lunch cold.

Somehow, time had crept up on her once again; the weekend was over and tomorrow was the start of another workweek. It was time for Sadie to fade into the background so Sarah could bring home the bacon. Casual office attire would cover her bruises, and tepid coworkers would replace her fierce roller derby sisterhood. *Too bad being Sadie didn't pay the bills*, Sarah ruefully sighed as she put away her gear and readied her satchel for work.

Her mother had originally given her the nickname, and for years, Sarah loathed it. It sounded so WASP and old-fashioned, like "would you like more pâté on the veranda before we play another round of badminton?" The fact that Sadie wasn't any shorter than her actual name—in number of letters or syllables—was doubly irritating. It became marginally cooler after she found out the Beatles used it in a song, but Sarah never really embraced it until she reclaimed it from her mother.

That was how Slashy Sadie was born. In many ways, she felt her alter ego had become her true self, and it was Sarah Pullman that was the pretense.

As she reached for her laptop, she fought off the urge to check her work e-mail before securing it in her bag. There was no point in getting ahead of what waited for her tomorrow, because there would just be another thing to take its place in an endless string of requests. She was unwilling to relinquish what was left of her evening to work; whatever was in there could wait until morning, when she was on the clock. After all, she didn't have to adult for another ten hours.

Sarah walked to her draft table, destined for the dumpster before she'd rescued and refurbished it. Now, it was a large flat surface for her to craft her designs—the pencil-to-paper kind reserved for her personal projects, not the drag-and-click ones that paid the bills. She rubbed the cascade of fabrics between her fingers and selected one from the stack. The material was slippery and it would be a pain to sew, but there was only one way to tell if it was "the one."

Sarah unfurled a few feet off the cardboard bolt with a familiar flick of the wrist and draped the swath across the dressmaker's mannequin beside the table. The adjustable dummy was her double in every way—same height and dimensions at the shoulder, bust, waist, and hip, and from shoulder-to-elbow and elbow-to-wrist. The only thing it was missing was a head, and that was hardly necessary for holding up clothing in progress.

Much to Sarah's delight and dismay, the midnight blue crêpe de chine hung just right. *I never make it easy on myself, do I?* she chided herself. Of course, she didn't mean it. Otherwise she wouldn't have purchased the fussy fabric at a remnant sale in the first place. She switched on a floor lamp, and a beacon of bright light flooded the otherwise dim room. As the iron heated up, she cleared the other rolls of material from the table and reset its tilt to neutral. She slid a large cutting mat over the surface and gathered her tools: pattern, fabric scissors, rotary cutter, and fabric weights.

The silky bolt unfurled with ease as Sarah measured the required length against the ruler on her mat. She placed the rectangle of Plexiglas on the mark and ran her rotary cutter along its edge, using her body weight to push the wheeled straight razor away from her. She locked the blade before carrying her selection to the ironing board where she gently worked out the creases on low heat, careful not to stretch the fabric in the process. She pulled the plug on the iron and gave her paper pattern a quick once over with the warm iron before it lost all its heat.

Safely deposited on the cutting surface, Sarah moved the pattern pieces around on the pressed material, imagining how she would have to cut and sew for the grain and seams to meet just so. It was a 2D-to-3D translation that all who sewed sewers eventually learned, sometimes the hard way. Once all the pieces of the pattern were strategically organized to minimize waste, Sarah dropped the weighted metal rings that would hold the pattern in place while she carefully cut out each piece. If the fabric had been more forgiving, she could have used pins and fabric scissors, but with crêpe de chine, the rotary cutter was the only way to get a true cut.

She became lost in precision as an ill wind blew in through a crack in the windowsill. The edges of the paper pattern rustled under the fabric weights as the wind crept deeper into her converted loft. Sarah shrugged off the chill as nothing more than another gust that broke through the shoddy insulation of her stylish but notoriously drafty abode.

She'd run her rotary cutter around all the pieces, but there were always stubborn spots that didn't quite cut through with the old blade. She kept meaning to buy a replacement, but it continually slipped further down her mental to-do list as something more pressing arose. Sarah extended her arm, blindly reaching out for her fabric scissors, the ornate ones shaped like a stork. She patted the table, fanning out her fingers to feel for the tool, but they failed to find purchase. When she turned her head, she spied a dark shadow cast over her outstretched arm and followed it to its origin. Her brown eyes widened, hardly believing what they saw.

If she had come to her senses sooner, perhaps she could have fought off her attacker, but such speculation became moot as the mortal remains of Sarah Pullman slumped onto her draft table, her blood seeping into the freshly cut swatches.

Chapter Two

Detroit, Michigan, USA
23rd of September, 3:45 p.m. (GMT-4)

Deep in the bowels of Zug Island, Teresa Maria Martinez—codename Lancer—sat in her subterranean office, laboring over her keyboard. Despite the lack of natural light, the room was adequately lit between the circular brass fixture mounted on the ceiling and the articulated desk lamp positioned between her two widescreen monitors. The saline walls absorbed the rapid staccato of her typing as she muttered to herself. After a busy week in the field, she'd spent the day catching up on her administrative work. She was determined to wrap up everything by the end of the day. However, her fingers struggled to keep up with her internal monologue.

Things had been busy since had Wilson vanished three weeks earlier. An investigation of his movements prior to his disappearance had led them to Siberia, but once he'd left the mortal realm, his trail went cold. Wherever Wilson was, he was still alive—the wards on the 500 were still active—and there was no evidence to suggest Ivory Tower had him. But it was a small consolation.

With one agent missing, everyone's workload had increased. As the newest agent, Martinez was kept closer to home and was generally the last to be sent abroad for missions. She was glad to give her passport a rest, but covering all local surveillance and interventions on her own was taxing. Luckily, she never backed down from a challenge.

Martinez paused and blinked her chestnut eyes a few times until the transient fuzziness in her vision cleared. The full spectrum bulbs were a vast improvement over the fluorescents that came with the office—last held by agent codename Patron—but hours at the computer were still hard on the eyes. She pulled her shoulders back and stretched her neck before focusing again on the monitors.

Unsurprising, spell check didn't recognize "rovalfairui," also known as a rust-wing faerie. A pair had crossed into the mortal realm and gotten loose in Detroit. While they were generally considered an avoidable nuisance in the Magh Meall, rovalfairui could cause untold damage in a world made of metal and steel. Unlike most fae, rovalfairui could not only touch cold iron without injury, they considered it a rare delicacy. As they were voracious eaters, the real danger in the mortal realm lay in a breeding pair. Without their native predators, it wouldn't take long for an infestation to take hold and exponentially worsen the problem.

Martinez had hunted them down to an abandoned factory. While most of the machinery had been scrapped long ago, there was always metallic debris and when that dried up, the structural supports. By the time she'd cornered them, they had gorged so much their tawny gossamer wings were no longer able to lift them into the air, making them significantly easier to target. But even with their grossly distended bellies, she still found them almost too pretty to shoot. She knew it was petty, but it made her happy that fae could get fat—a serious blow to such haughty, vain creatures. Lancer dispatched them back to the land of the fae, and once she was sure there was no hidden brood secreted away in the dark corners of the old factory, went home herself.

With a few clicks, Martinez added "rovalfairui" to her dictionary, and a sea of red underlines disappeared. *Isn't the first new entry, and won't be the last*, she thought as she rubbed her temples for the final bit—the expense report.

Even though the Salt Mine was a secret black ops agency tasked to monitor and manage supernatural activity, that didn't absolve the agents from filing paperwork. Just like FBI agents had to account for every bullet discharged from their weapon at the scene, Salt Mine agents had to account for every use of magic—how much, how was it used, and was it commensurate to the threat as perceived in the moment.

Agents would be compensated for expenditures deemed reasonable, using a set of algorithms based on historic estimations adjusted for inflation—which Martinez found hilarious—to help agents offset accrued karmic debt. Those deemed excessive but ultimately helpful to the mission received partial recompense. Any deemed unnecessary were the agent's responsibility. For an organization funded by dark money siphoned from both the CIA and FBI and property confiscated from malevolent practitioners, they were ridiculously penurious with reimbursing karmic mileage.

Expense reports were also used to keep track of equipment use: either spent, damaged, or destroyed. This helped Harold Weber—quartermaster and Salt Mine inventor extraordinaire—keep tabs on inventory. That's why getting the incident report right was so important. Capturing a true picture of what happened for future reference was a noble intent, but justification of and compensation for arcane resource use was a much stronger motivation.

Martinez filled in the cells of the standardized form: ten salt casts, ritual scrying (eye of the needle), one casting of true sight, two castings of immobilize, two banishment bullets (North America). She scanned her narrative for typos and missing words her brain had filled in but her fingers had missed. Once she was certain it supported her use of magic, Martinez sent the file to the appropriate department on the intranet with a few clicks.

With the die cast, she allowed herself to relax; that last one wasn't too bad, but the longer and more convoluted a case got, the harder it was to pull everything together. Martinez cleared her desk and started winding everything down. She removed today's dailies to make way for tomorrow's, shut down her computer, and packed up her things. Just before she was about to turn off the lights, Martinez reached over and stroked a delicate buttercup petal of the potted Narcissus flower on her desk, her purloined souvenir from the Magh Meall.

Once upon a time, Martinez had known that faeries were the stuff of children's stories, magic was little more than slight-of-hand and expensive props, and demons and devils were allegorical creatures evoked to elicit obedience to the religious structure of the time. She'd allowed that they all had a place and purpose in human consciousness, but they couldn't be real. Until that fateful day she found out that they were.

All things considered, Martinez had taken it in stride, and ten months in, she almost felt like she had found her footing at her new job. She was grateful for Wilson's tutelage in those early days, but it wasn't until these past few months that she'd had her first real taste of being a Salt Mine agent. When Wilson was around and just across the hall, she'd still felt like she was on probation, but with him gone, she had to stand on her own two feet or fall flat on her face.

Of course, she wasn't entirely on her own. She had Chloe and Dot, the conjoined twins that ran the Salt Mine's esoteric library, and Weber kept her well-supplied and always made time for her inquiries. Martinez was pleasantly surprised to discover not all the Salt Mine Agents were as anti-social as Wilson. And then there was Stigma.

Officially, Alexander James Husnik died five years ago battling a wendigo, and Stigma's deep cover, Petty Officer Boris Mikhailovich Petrov, drowned last month in the waters west of Sal Island, Cape Verde with the rest of the crew of the *Yantar*, a Russian naval vessel renowned as a spy ship in the intelligence community. So when David LaSalle deposited Stigma on her doorstep with no formal identity and a broken leg, she wasn't sure how long he was going to be there or how well they would get along. Martinez never quite mastered the art of cohabitation, platonic or otherwise, but she didn't have the heart to leave him convalescing in the Salt Mine. He would still be housebound, but at least it was in a real home.

There was only so much of doing nothing that Stigma could take, and two weeks into his convalescence, he'd started helping out more. He had already deepcleaned the house. Twice. He had changed all the burnt-out bulbs and tightened every loose screw he could find on a handle, cabinet, or door. With his help, Martinez now had a fully stocked ritual room behind the secret panel in the basement. He did the dishes as soon as they hit the sink and emptied the hamper regularly. Given the right seasoning mixes, Stigma wasn't a half-bad cook. Martinez had come to understand why so many men sought out a full-time housewife.

After some adjustments, they negotiated a workable routine. He fended for himself while Martinez was at work, and she picked up groceries and supplies until he finally had a new permanent alias with a working bank account. He kept her general hours and used the ritual room in the basement while she was at work so it would be free when she was home. Luckily, there were two full bathrooms in the house.

She, in turn, acknowledged his need for engagement and social interaction. While the three resident ghosts adored Stigma, they could only manifest for brief stints during the day, and the only living people that knew he was alive were all Salt Mine, who were all too busy holding down the fort to visit with any regularity. Martinez loaded him up with books, games, and whatever hobby materials he asked for. They often ate dinner together, watched TV, or worked on her magical practice.

Magic was so personal and intuitive to Stigma, just an extension of himself. Martinez didn't have that facility and ease with casting yet; it was something *other*, something to be studied in a didactic way. That was how Chloe and Dot approached it, and she'd never felt close enough to Wilson to probe his process, only observe it from a distance. With Stigma's guidance, she was learning to become comfortable and familiar with magic, the arcane equivalent of developing an intimate knowledge of one's weapon—when you need to use it, you want it to feel second nature.

Martinez switched off the lights and her mid-century-chic office dimmed in the glow of the cooling bulbs. She pulled her office door shut and glanced down the hallway of mostly empty offices. It harkened back to a time when the Salt Mine had dozens of agents instead of the current eight—with one missing and one injured and technically dead. She cruised down the ramp to the elevators and presented her palm and retina for scanning—a requirement if she wanted the elevator to go anywhere.

On the ride up to the first floor, Martinez absentmindedly rubbed the amber pendent Weber had given her before her first foray into the field. It was designed to absorb magic directed against the wearer, and she had taken to always wearing it, along with the pendant of Saint Michael and the crucifix gifted to her by her mother. Now that she was spending more time in the field solo, she would take all the help she could get.

When the elevator doors opened, Angela Abrams came into view, perched behind a wall of clear ballistic glass. Abrams was the Salt Mine's gatekeeper—no one came in or out without her clearance. She leaned over and spoke into the microphone. "You know the drill, Martinez," the blonde instructed over the tinny speaker. Martinez gave a half smile and loaded her possessions into the slot. There was a time when she considered the in-and-out procedure overkill, but after she got a glimpse of some of the items stored in the depths of the Salt Mine, she understood the precaution.

"Taking off a little early?" Abrams quizzed the agent as they waited for the machine to do its job.

"Came in a little early." Martinez shrugged. "Six of one,

half dozen of the other." Her tone was polite without inviting conversation.

Abrams sensed there was no impending gossip coming her way and returned to her reading. Once the scan chimed all clear, Abrams pressed a series of buttons and the door opened. "Have a good evening."

Martinez picked up her bag and curtly nodded. "You, too."

"Only one more elevator to freedom," Martinez sighed under her breath. Tonight was Stigma's turn to cook dinner—tacos, based on the groceries he had her pick up yesterday—and she would have the luxury of sitting back and relaxing once she got home. She was one short commute away from a cold beer.

Martinez brushed an errant wisp of hair from her eyes as she stowed her bag and climbed into her pitch black Hellcat. She rued the day she let Stigma talk her into getting bangs. With the press of a button, the engine purred on ignition—the sound made her toes curl in delight. She was never able to really open it up on the route from Zug Island to her home in Corktown, but it was always a pleasure to drive.

When Martinez entered the house, the chorus of "Take a Chance on Me" was blaring from the speakers. She closed the door behind her and put her leather bag down, securing her weapon, badge, and ID. "I'm home," she called out.

"You're early," a familiar voice hollered from the kitchen over the music. "I've just started prepping."

"That's okay. I'm not hungry yet," she reassured him. "But

I could use a drink." When she entered the kitchen, Stigma was tying apron strings with his crutches propped against the counter. He looked patently silly in her "Latina AF" apron, swaying on one leg to '70s Swedish pop.

He looked up. "Any word?" he asked. She knew there was only one thing he could mean: Wilson's whereabouts.

Martinez shook her head. "Not yet, but the wards are still up." Stigma nodded solemnly. She lightened the mood with a light jab and a glace toward the speakers. "But now I know what you are really doing while I'm at work," she teased as she passed him on her way for a beer. She popped the top with the magnetic church key that resided on the fridge. "I'm officially judging you."

Stigma feigned indignation and emphatically stated, "Everyone loves Abba." He shook his head and switched to Russian, "*I ežu ponjatno!*" Literally, *even a hedgehog understands*, idiomatically meaning it's a no-brainer.

Martinez drew a long sip of her cold hefeweizen before she replied in kind, "*Durakov ne sejut, ne žnut, sami rodjatsja.*" No one makes fools, but yet they're everywhere.

He laughed out loud and grinned impishly; it made his brown eyes squint. His short crew cut had grown out and the bronze tan he'd acquired over years at sea had faded to his natural pale hazelnut now that he wasn't under constant sun. After weeks of reduced activity and good eating, a thin layer of padding now covered his lean muscles. Other than the cast on his right leg, the past six weeks had been good to him.

Stigma pushed some produce her way along with the cutting board. "Make yourself useful and help me chop onions and peppers."

Chapter Three

Detroit, Michigan, USA
23rd of September, 9:35 p.m. (GMT-4)

Detective Marshall Collins was on his way home when he got the call from his partner—a body on the other side of town. He double-checked the address she'd sent him and looked for a good spot to turn around. He blindly groped the floorboard for his emergency vehicle light, and once in place, flipped the switch. The flashing blue and red cleared an adequate path through traffic and he forewent the siren. It wasn't like the body was going to get any more dead.

He glanced down at the warm cheesesteak sandwich wrapped in foil on his passenger seat; he knew he should have eaten it there instead of taking it to go. Assuming he was actually going to make it home to eat a warm meal was hubris on his part, and his inner cynic knew better than to tempt fate.

He allowed himself to grouse in hopes of purging his dourness before he arrived on scene. Jen had been making more "grumpy old man" references as of late and damned if she wasn't a little right. He had been feeling the weight of his twenty years in homicide after the spate of suspicious deaths last month—six in as many days. They stopped almost as suddenly as they'd started. They weren't the goriest of ends, but something about them stuck with Collins. Thanks to the FBI, they were all taken off Detroit PD's caseload but not from his mind. Maybe he would put in for some time off…

As the other squad cars came into view, Collins told himself to buck up, which was as close as he ever got to a pep talk. He nodded as he passed some uniforms and spied his partner interviewing a distraught woman just outside the secured perimeter. Detective Jennifer Cerova was no waif, but compared to the strapping blonde beside her, she seemed downright diminutive. Collins pegged the crying Valkyrie for at least six feet tall and if her developed traps were any indication, she could probably bench him.

He slowed his pace to give Cerova time to note his approach. Cerova gave Collins a slight nod, signaling him to stay back. Collins knew his partner well enough that she was onto something and didn't want any distractions. Collins halted his advance and found a uniform on the periphery to engage while picking up snippets of Cerova's conversation.

"When was the last time you saw or spoke to Ms. Pullman?" Cerova asked neutrally.

The towering woman daubed her blue eyes with a crumpled tissue. "She was at practice last night, but that ended around eight."

"Did anything seem out of the ordinary?" Cerova nudged without leading.

"It was just a regular practice. She took a nasty spill, but that's hardly unusual. We compete hard and train harder," she answered the detective.

"Any communication with Ms. Pullman since then? Texts, social media, calls?" Cerova reiterated for clarity. She was used to going over things two or three times to extract a full account.

The twin braids swayed down the Valkyrie's back as she shook her head. "I tried texting her when she didn't show tonight, but she never replied. That's how I knew something was wrong. She would never miss a meeting and not let someone know."

Cerova made affirming gestures as she flipped through her notes. "Do you know of anyone who would want to hurt Sarah?" Collins noticed her sudden personalization of the victim, a tactic used to knock witnesses off kilter to see what shakes out.

"I've known Sadie for years and I can't imagine anyone wanting to hurt her. She's a rock—the first person to lend a hand when someone's in trouble." Cerova noted the alternate name.

"Any recent personality changes you noticed, or concerns Sadie mentioned to you in passing or in confidence?" Cerova prodded gently.

There was a weighted pause before the blonde answered, "None that I can think of."

Cerova was certain there was more there to probe, but she

left the seed planted and would wait to see what fruit it bore. "If something comes to mind, no matter how small, don't hesitate to notify us. You never know what could help us find who did this to Sadie." Cerova leaned in heavily before flagging down a uniformed officer. "You'll understand why we have to keep your copy of the keys to Ms. Pullman's place. If you'll leave your contact information with Officer Thompson, you're free to go, Ms. Holt."

"Why do you need my information?" Holt asked acutely.

Cerova stared her down with her dark brown eyes. "In case we need to ask you further questions. This is a police investigation, and we may need to revisit witnesses as more information comes to light."

An odd smile broke out on the blonde's face. "Right, of course."

Collin's smirked at the exchange. Cerova may have been half a foot shorter and twenty plus years his junior, but moments like this disabused him of any notions that she wasn't cut out to be a homicide detective. Collins approached his partner and held up the crime scene tape for her to pass under.

"About time," Cerova needled him as she sashayed under the yellow tape.

Collins shrugged. "I had a hot date."

Cerova squinted—it was Monday night. "Lefty's?"

"Best cheesesteak that doesn't require me to actually be in Philly," he snarked. He waited until the blonde was out of earshot. "Wanna fill me in?"

"Deceased is Sarah Pullman, thirty-seven years old. Found dead a little over an hour ago by Caroline Holt after Pullman missed a league organizational meeting for Detroit Roller Derby. Last seen alive yesterday evening at practice at 8:00 p.m. She worked as a graphic designer for a local advertising firm but we still haven't confirmed whether she made it to work today. Divorced but lived alone. Neighbors didn't hear or see anything suspicious. Uniforms found no signs of forced entry. Forensic team is inside now."

"And who is Caroline Holt to Sarah Pullman?" Collins inquired.

"Platonic friend, self-described derby wife," she replied as she motioned toward the stairs. "We're on the top floor."

"Do I want to know what a derby wife is?" Collins queried as they climbed the steps and gloved up.

"It's like a work wife—the person who has your back and makes sure you don't have lettuce in your teeth after lunch. Except in derby, it's the woman who goes to the ER with you when you break something and holds your hair when you're puking at the after party," she patiently answered. "I'm surprised you didn't ask me what roller derby is."

"Hey, I saw the Drew Barrymore movie," he said defensively as they neared Pullman's front door.

Cerova snorted. "You know that movie is at least a decade old."

"Drew Barrymore is timeless," he affirmed.

Cerova let him have this one and they crossed the threshold. "Let's see what Doug's uncovered."

Pullman lived on the top floor of a manufacturing facility that had been rezoned and refurbished for residential purpose sometime in the '90s. The vaulted ceiling was fifteen feet at its peak, and tall windows lined the lone wall that exposed the original brick. The furnishings were an eclectic mix that favored age and style over newness. There was nothing out-of-the-box from IKEA or Target in here.

Advertised as an open floor plan, the loft only had three rooms: a bathroom, a bedroom, and one giant room for everything else. Thus, the whole of the crime scene came into view upon clearing the entryway. In one corner, a lean figure was buckled over the table. Under her were crimson-stained paper patterns and saturated fabric that had absorbed as much of her blood as it could. The rest had flowed to the floor, now a sticky burgundy pool. Pullman was a slight thing compared to the Scandinavian brick Cerova had just interviewed; the fact they both skated on the same team seemed unreal.

Douglas Knoll, Wayne Country medical examiner, popped his head up from the corpse. "Detectives, come on over and take a look at what I found." He labeled a bagged piece of evidence before handing it off to an assistant. "Allow me to introduce you to Sarah Pullman, aka Slashy Sadie, #96 of the Motor City Rollers and arguable one of the most nimble blockers in the league."

"Why am I not surprised you're a fan?" Collins sardonically remarked.

"Full-contact sport on roller skates played by women in fishnets—what about that doesn't sound up my alley?" Knoll retorted.

Clowns to the left of me, jokers to the right, Cerova bemoaned internally. "You got a time of death?"

"Based on ambient temperature, liver temp, and level of rigidity," Knoll qualified, "my best guess is longer than twelve hours but no more than a day."

"A twelve-hour window? You gotta give us something better than that," Collins pressed.

"If I had to shave off for a tighter estimate, I would say she died earlier rather than later." He consulted his watch and did the math. "Between 9:00 p.m. to 3:00 a.m. For what its worth, the lamp was still on when we got here." Cerova jotted it down in her notes.

"And cause of death?" Collins joined in.

"On first blush, the pair of scissors sticking out of her chest. It's lodged in there deep and she's not a very big person. I'd wager it punctured something vital—heart or lungs—and she bled out quickly. No signs of struggle in the apartment or defensive wounds on her arms and hands. She's got one hell of a goose egg on her right thigh, but based on the coloration, I would wager it was when she was still alive." Knoll drew back

Pullman's dangling robe to expose the fresh bruise.

"She may have gotten that at practice, but we'll have to confirm that with her other teammates," Cerova added.

"I'll know more after I finish the autopsy, but I suspect this was the one and only strike and she was down for the count. The absence of arterial spray suggests the stabbing implement was not taken out after hitting pay dirt. Obviously, I'll run a tox screen to see if she was chemically subdued beforehand."

Collins did a quick visual sweep of the room. Pullman's wallet, laptop, and electronics were all in plain sight and still here. "It doesn't look like a robbery."

"There's a good chance it's personal," Cerova commented. "People don't generally let strangers get this close to them without a struggle, especially in their own home after dark."

"It takes a lot to stab someone with enough force to kill on the first try," Collins agreed with his partner.

"Figuring out the whys and hows is your job," Knoll concluded as he stepped aside, clearing a path for his team to move the body. "I'll get her back to the morgue and see what I can find."

A quiet calm came over the detectives amid the rapid camera clicks that captured the scene and the original location of any bagged evidence they'd collected. Knoll knew that tacit tautness well—they were already plotting a strategy to track down the perpetrator.

There was always the chance for a random psycho, but more

often than not, victims knew their attackers in some capacity. It was a terrifying truth people avoided acknowledging because it made the world a less friendly place in their head. In a case like this, it was a matter of breaking down Pullman's points of connection and her routine.

They would conduct a proper investigation and follow the evidence, but they each had their own theories. Collins wondered just how recently Pullman had been divorced and the circumstances of the decoupling. Intimate partner violence was ubiquitous, and it was the kind of simmering anger that needed little provocation to boil over. Cerova wanted to know what Caroline Holt wasn't telling her and if anyone else besides her derby wife had a key to Pullman's place.

Chapter Four

Detroit, Michigan, USA
24th of September, 7:20 p.m. (GMT-4)

Caroline Holt awoke in her cool, dark bedroom, uncertain of the time. Before she went to bed, she had drawn all the blinds and unhooked the light-blocking curtains in hopes it would help her migraine. She groped for her phone and found the weighted facemask instead. She surmised she had been out for some time—it was no longer cold. Finally, she found her phone and checked the date and time. Her eyes squinted at the screen; the light still smarted, but not as badly. It no longer felt like an ice pick gouging into her skull.

As the fog of sleep slowly cleared, Holt suddenly remembered that Sadie was dead. Her eyes were puffy and sore from all the crying and her bed was littered with crumpled tissues. She'd scolded herself all night—she should have asked more questions. She knew Sadie wasn't acting like herself, but she'd figured it had something to do with her ex remarrying. That was enough to drive anyone a little cuckoo; even when you didn't want them back, it still stung when they moved on. But then everything seemed fine once they started training again. Derby had a way of doing that—it might not fix everything, but it made you stronger to handle the crap life threw at you.

Holt untangled her long limbs from the sheets and gulped the glass of water on her nightstand. She went to the bathroom and downed a second—she was so thirsty, and the last thing she needed was a rebound headache from dehydration. She hadn't had a full-blown migraine in almost a year. She was so good about avoiding triggers and catching them early, but this one came out of nowhere, hit hard, and played dirty.

She needed food, something simple that wouldn't cause the nausea to return and didn't require her to cook. She always kept a few cans of chicken noodle soup and saltine crackers for just such contingencies. The thought of sunlight still hurt, even the oblique rays just before dusk. She turned on a floor lamp to the lowest setting as she walked to the kitchen, hazarding soft, low light. That's when she saw it on her coffee table—Sadie's journal. An entirely different set of memories and panic flooded Holt, and she quickly took a seat on the couch.

In her mind's eye, she could see it play out, like watching a movie from behind her own eyes. Sadie had missed the planning meeting for Junior Derby and wasn't answering any of her texts. After the meeting, Holt swung by her place to check on her and tried knocking repeatedly. When no one answered, she fished out the copy of the key Sadie had given her "for emergencies." As soon as she opened the door, she knew everything was terribly wrong.

Holt didn't scream or cry out. Instead, she closed the door

behind her. Sadie's apartment was on the top floor, so there wouldn't be much through traffic, but she didn't want anyone to see what was inside. Not yet.

As soon as Holt had seen all that blood, she knew Sadie was gone. No one could lose that much blood and still be alive. This was the scene of a crime and it would be wrong to take the journal. How many court proceedings had she committed to record? Tampering with a crime scene was bad news. And yet she grabbed the notebook and stashed it in her trunk under some blankets before calling 911. Her first instinct was to run, but she knew notifying the authorities would buy her some goodwill and time; she wouldn't dare report the body if she had done anything wrong.

Once the police arrived, the waves of adrenaline crested and fell. Holt had done her best to stay focused and answer their questions directly without offering excessive information. Thankfully, the stress of finding your friend dead could account for many things. Her growing anxiety kept waiting for the police to search her car, while her rational mind argued such a thing was unlikely—she wasn't a suspect.

The drive home had felt like an eternity. She'd stuffed the purloined notebook into a cloth grocery bag and brought it inside. It wasn't until she had barricaded herself inside her apartment that her legs gave out and reality had set in. She might not have anything to do with Sadie's death, but she was no longer innocent.

After she'd regained her footing, she immediately checked all the latches and locks, including the keyless deadlock on the front door—jiggling each exactly three times to make sure they were securely fastened. She kept the lights off; she didn't want anyone to know she was home. Then she called into work and left a message on her supervisor's voicemail—she was taking a personal day.

Once she'd cocooned herself in the safety of her home, there was only one thing left to do: read the journal. What was so important that Sadie would make her promise to take it if something were to happen to her? As Holt flipped through the leather-bound book, she recognized nascent concepts for new formations and plays on the flat track among the pages as well as designs for clothing and costumes with columns of sums and maths in the margins. There were plenty of drawings, doodles, sketches, and notes—a place for Sadie to hash out ideas. And then there were pages of schematics and equations Holt couldn't begin to fathom. That was when the migraine came on.

She remembered taking her migraine pills last night, despite how much she hated how drugged-out she felt afterwards—like having a hangover without any of the fun of drinking. But experience had taught her not to wait; it was easier to abort a migraine earlier rather than later. Usually they worked within thirty minutes, an hour tops, but the more she'd tried to concentrate on Sadie's curly scrawl and penciled drawings, the more her head throbbed. Once the nausea came and the auras were floating across her vision, she'd shut the journal and pulled her weighted mask out of the freezer. She had already taken as many pills as she could without any sign of relief in sight. At times like that, she had two options: sleep it off or go to the emergency room for a shot of Toradol, since all the urgent cares would be closed.

As Holt pieced together the past twenty-four hours, her mind raced. None of it made sense—she knew better! But in the moment, she'd had such clarity. A promise was a promise, and that was what Sadie had asked her to do. What was done could not be undone. The question was what she should do next. She could come clean with the cops, but there would be no guarantee that she wouldn't be charged, and that would put her job at risk.

The blonde took a deep breath and centered herself again. *No, there was a reason Sadie wanted it out of her place, and knowing her, she wouldn't leave me in the dark*, she reassured herself. She reached for the notebook but hesitated with a visceral recoil, not unlike shying away from something hot after being burned. She had no reasonable explanation, but she was scared to touch it again. "Get your shit together, Caroline," she chastised herself. "It's just a book."

With her courage summoned, she flipped the cover open but dared not go any further. There was a series of numbers written on the bottom corner, enough to be a phone number.

Holt picked up her cell phone and dialed. She counted the seconds between rings and almost hung up after the third, when someone finally picked up the other end. It was a male voice, deep but not gruff. Holt cleared her throat and spoke, "Hello. I'm calling to inform you that Sarah Pullman has been killed. I think she wanted me to call you if something bad happen to her."

*****

"No, that is not how you make a sponge!" Stigma leaned forward and yelled at the television. "That cake is going to be so flat—how's he going to slice three layers out of that?"

Martinez smirked. "Two seasons of Great British Bake Off and you're a master baker?"

Stigma sat back on the couch and readjusted his elevated right leg. "I know the lightness in a sponge cake comes from aerating the eggs, and stirring the flour in like that is just going to knock out all the air."

Her phone lit up and buzzed on the coffee table. A name flashed on the screen: Aloysius Hardwick, magician and owner of 18 is 9, Detroit's premier goth dance club. Martinez had become his de facto handler after Wilson's disappearance, and numbers were exchanged. Not that Hardwick knew of Salt Mine's predicament—he was the worst gossip and traded in secrets and favors. As far as Hardwick knew, Martinez was simply taking over for Wilson, which would have suited Wilson just fine.

Stigma paused the program as Martinez picked up her phone and answered, "This is Teresa."

"Hi. It's Aloysius. I'm in a pickle." He was unusually curt, and his voice lacked the silk and luster he usually affected.

"Define pickle," she inquired as she motioned to Stigma that he could continue watching without her. She rose from the couch and went to the kitchen.

Hardwick lowered his voice and answered somberly, "I have a non-practitioner sitting in my office with a magically booby-trapped book claiming that it may have something to do with her friend's death."

Martinez shrugged; she'd heard worse. "Makes sense. She's out of her depth and goes to the club for help." It was a well-known fact in some circles that 18 is 9 was a haven for practitioners of the arts. "I'm assuming her friend was a practitioner?"

"No idea. I don't know either of them," he stated plainly.

Her brow furrowed. "Then how did this woman find you? The club doesn't open for another two hours." Hardwick had security out the wazoo, and Martinez had experienced firsthand how challenging it was to get in during non-business hours.

"Ah, that's the interesting bit. My private number was written in her friend's book," he replied mysteriously. Martinez took that as a good sign—he was spooked, but not so much that he ceased seeing the drama in it all.

"Keep her there. I'll be there in twenty minutes," she answered, already making her mental list of gear to grab before she left the house.

"Great! I'll let the boys know to expect you." His voice lighted with relief. He casually added as an aside, "You might want to take it easy on the badge. *Technically*, she took the book from a crime scene."

Martinez shook her head and rolled her eyes. *What are you getting me into, Aloysius?*

Chapter Five

Detroit, Michigan, USA
24th of September, 8:25 p.m. (GMT-4)

Martinez pulled into the near-empty parking lot of 18 is 9 in the warehouse district and double-checked the contents of her bag before exiting the Hellcat. She dressed casually in jeans and a light sweater with a black leather jacket—not exactly club wear, but something more approachable than her standard office attire. She'd let her hair down and wore little to no makeup to soften her appearance for Hardwick's perplexing visitor.

She rapped on the reinforced metal door, and the muscle on the other side gave her entrance as soon as she gave her name. Another bodyguard radioed her arrival as he led her to the stairwell behind another locked and manned door. "Mr. Hardwick is expecting you on the second floor," he politely informed her.

Martinez climbed the stairs and readied a spell—you only have one chance to make a first impression. *Hail Mary, full of grace...* She opened the door into the cozy second-floor lounge. It looked much the same as the last time she was here, except Hardwick had company.

The blonde woman pacing in front of the fireplace was tall but not lanky. She was wide at the shoulders and hips with a thick waist—fit, not fat. Her long hair was pulled back in a ponytail, granting full view of her delicate complexion and prominent cheekbones. By the looks of it, she had had a rough couple of days—her eyes were swollen and puffy, her shoulders slumped forward, and the triangular wrinkles between her eyes were set in place.

"You made it!" Aloysius greeted her warmly while the blonde just looked startled. "Caroline, this is the woman I was telling you about. If something in this book is connected to your friend's death, she'll be able to figure it out."

Martinez held out her hand and released her will. "I'm Teresa. I'm sorry to hear about your loss."

Holt took her hand and a soothing wave rolled over her from their contact. The furrows in her brow lessened—this was someone who would listen and understand. "Caroline. It's nice to meet you," she replied out of habit.

Martinez gave her a warm smile and released her grip. "Aloysius gave me the broad strokes over the phone, but I would very much like to hear what happened in your own words. Why don't we sit down and get comfortable?" She let Holt pick her seat first before selecting the place on the couch that would allow her to observe Holt without being confrontational. Martinez spied a leather-bound book on the table. "Was that your friend's?" Holt confirmed with a terse nod. "I want to reassure you that I'm not interested in *how* you acquired this book so much as I want to understand why it was so important to your friend." Holt bobbed her head again.

She turned her head and met Hardwick's gaze. "Ali, I think we have everything we need up here. Why don't you check on the club for a bit and give us privacy—girl talk and all that." Her tone and smile were friendly enough, but Hardwick deduced it wasn't a request. She had never called him Ali before, and Martinez was hardly the type of woman to evoke "girl talk." And then, there was the intensity behind the mirth in her eyes.

He grinned. "Of course," he agreed and graciously retreated by means of the elevator.

Once the doors shut behind him, Martinez turned her attention back to Holt. "Now, I want you to start at the beginning and don't leave anything out." She tilted her head and leaned in while Caroline Holt gave her account, nodding and making little noises of affirmation every so often. Martinez watched her body language, her facial expressions, and word choice. On balance, she was inclined to believe that this woman believed what she was saying.

"And that's how I got here," Holt concluded.

Martinez consulted the few notes she'd scribbled. "I'd like you to tell me more about this promise," she started. "When exactly did this take place?"

Holt was confused by the direction Martinez took, but summoned her memories nonetheless. "It was earlier this summer, sometime in June. I took Sadie out to dinner to get her mind off her ex's wedding, and afterwards, we were drinking wine at her place."

"How did the promise come up in conversation?"

Holt took her time, trying to get the details right. "Sadie didn't want Jason back so much as she was sad he'd found someone else. In her mind, if he could be happy with this new woman, it was an indictment against her…like she was the problem all along." Holt wanted to be fair to her friend despite being dead. Martinez could respect that.

"Anyway, I listened and told her in the nicest way possible that it was bullshit. That two perfectly fine people could be terrible as a couple. It's about incompatibility, not culpability. She rebutted that either way, she was all alone. Then I reminded her that she had me and the rest of the derby girls." Holt's body relaxed and her gestures became more spontaneous. Martinez welcomed her growing trust. "That's when she asked me… if something were to happen to her, would I make sure her journal was safe."

Martinez couldn't think of a better way to say it, so she left it vague. "This is going to sound weird, but did you and Sadie exchange bodily fluid during this conversation?"

Holt looked at her quizzically. "Like spitting on your hand and shaking on it?"

"Or pricking a finger," Martinez added.

"No, and we didn't pinky swear, either," Holt said with

some levity. It was the closest she had come to a smile in the past forty-eight hours. "But she did make me say it out loud."

"Like a pronouncement?" Martinez suggested.

"Sort of," she agreed after some hemming and hawing. The blonde sat up straight and her voice shifted officiously, "I, Caroline Holt, promise you, Sarah Pullman, that in the event that something happens to you, I will ensure the safety of your journal." Holt returned to her normal posture and speaking voice, "It's sort of a joke between us because I'm a court reporter and I can drop some legalese at a moment's notice. I swear, lawyers get paid by the word and letter."

Martinez mulled it over. *That might be enough for a binding oath*. She folded her hands in her lap and broached the next subject cautiously. "If the only thing you did wrong was take the journal, you aren't going to get in trouble for that with me, but if there is something else you feel you should add, now is the time to do it."

"Like what?" Holt asked honestly.

"Did you take or move anything else from Sadie's apartment after you found the body?" she asked neutrally.

"No," Holt answered without hesitation.

"Did she give you anything in the days, weeks, or months preceding her death?" Martinez suggested.

The blonde shook her head. "Not that I can think of. We were always lending each other the same twenty dollars, but no gifts."

Martinez threw it out there, "Was she acting differently? Any departure from routine?" When Holt didn't immediately answer in the negative, Martinez added, "The more I know, the more I can help."

"I don't want you to think anyone at the Derby is involved, because that's bananas, but Sadie was spending a lot more time at the drill hall this summer," Holt conceded.

Martinez perked up. "Tell me more about the drill hall."

"As you know, Sadie and I met each other through derby, and the drill hall is home to Detroit Roller Derby. It's where we hold local games and special events."

"From what you said earlier, it sounds like Sadie was really active in derby, not just as a skater but in the administration of the league," Martinez challenged her obliquely.

"Except that summer is our off-season, and the Masonic Temple was doing repairs on the drill hall," Holt countered.

"Do you have any idea what Sadie was doing at the drill hall?"

Holt shrugged. "Not a clue, but when I went to clear out my locker for the summer, I caught her once using one of those clicking measuring wheels they use to mark fields."

"A perambulator?"

"I think that's what it's called," Holt responded, unsure if that was the right word. "Which again doesn't make sense. We've used that space for years, and the track is already marked."

"Could the repairs have damaged the flooring?" Martinez

wagered a guess.

"I don't think so," Holt replied dubiously. "They're renovating the ceiling back to the original 1920 design. The floors should have been covered and protected."

"Caroline, if Sadie was hanging around the drill hall during off season, why are you so certain that no one at the derby is involved?" Martinez pointed out the incongruity.

Holt paused to find the right words, and Martinez left the lull undisturbed. The skater eventually spoke. "We're a family—not the biological kind that are accidents of birth, but a chosen family. It takes too much hard work and dedication for casual interest, and people who don't *really* want to be there are sifted out pretty quickly. We may compete against each other and we certainly don't always get along, but we would never hurt each other," she stated emphatically.

Holt's earnest sincerity was so raw that Martinez averted her gaze and broke eye contact. In that the brief respite, Holt took a good look at the woman who sat with her. She might not be cop, but she was something. Her appearance and demeanor were casual, but her style of questioning and train of thought reminded Holt of law enforcement from all the time she had spent in court.

"If you don't mind me asking, who exactly are you?" Holt gingerly inquired. She was surprised that the question hadn't come up sooner.

Martinez put down her notes. "What did Aloysius tell

you?"

The blonde shrugged. "He was pretty vague on details, only that you definitely weren't a cop and you could take care of the journal."

"Well, considering the circumstances of our meeting, perhaps vague is the best course of action," Martinez posited. "Let's just say that if Sadie was killed for whatever is in that journal, I'll be able to keep it safe until the killer is found." Martinez touched the blonde's arm and streamed a thin thread of her will. "So you can consider your promise fulfilled."

Holt's shoulders dropped two inches and a look of calm came over her face.

"I'll see what I can uncover. Until I know more, if anyone asks, we never met. Deal?"

Holt appraised her interlocutor. "Deal," she agreed. "Should we spit and shake on it?" she joked.

Martinez let out a soft laugh. "Go home, get some rest. I'll take care of this." She motioned to the book on the table. "If you remember anything else, call me." She presented Holt an unlabeled card with a number that would reroute to her mobile. "If you feel in danger—"

"Wait," Holt interrupted. "Why would I be in danger?"

"If someone killed Sadie for what is in her journal, anyone who had contact with it could be at risk. Now that I have it, it probably won't be an issue, but I would be remiss if I didn't at least mention it as a possibility. So if you feel like someone is following you or you feel like you are being watched, call me. If you can't get a hold of me and it's dire, come to 18 is 9. Aloysius has a soft spot for damsels in distress."

Holt snorted. At six-foot-two and 180 pounds, she had never considered herself as someone in need of saving. Martinez pulled out a plastic sack from her bag and reached for the book on the table.

"Be careful with that thing," Holt said suspiciously.

Martinez smiled. "Of course. Now, let's get out of here before the DJ starts the music."

Chapter Six

Detroit, Michigan, USA
24th of September, 11:50 p.m. (GMT-4)

Parked across the street from Sarah Pullman's apartment, Martinez kept vigil in the dark through a pair of night vision binoculars. The evening was still, and she hadn't seen nor heard any evidence of resident dogs nearby. With Pullman's journal safely packed in salt at her warded house in Corktown, Martinez felt it was only prudent to take a look at the scene of the crime. If there was nothing esoteric of note, perhaps this was simply a case for Detroit PD. After all, there wasn't anything inherently mysterious about death by stabbing.

By her reckoning, it'd been over twenty-four hours since the police found the body. The detectives and crime scene investigators should have picked through everything and gone home, but the crime scene tape would still be in place—the perfect time for her to sneak in and investigate magically. Martinez had her gloves, gear, Glock, and—just in case she had to justify her presence—her FBI ID, although her intent was not to be caught.

She checked her watch and confirmed that the windows from the neighboring units went dark an hour ago. They should be fast asleep now. She exited her Hellcat and made her approach. Dressed in all black, she kept to the shadows and silently climbed the stairs to the loft. Yellow tape hung diagonally across the frame, and the porch fixture beside the door was dark. Luckily, Martinez didn't need light to work.

She cast out a bead of will, checking for wards, but all she found was a light protection emanating from the rosemary wreath hanging on the door—the magical equivalent of a "No Solicitation" sign. She pulled out her picks, and one by one, the tumblers fell into place under her dexterous touch. When she felt the lock release, she turned the knob with her gloved hand and entered.

The apartment was lit by moonlight cascading in through the wall of large windows set in brick. Martinez pulled out her mini-flashlight and saltcaster and started in the main room. Systematically working clockwise, she searched while she waited for the blown salt to settle. Everything had been rifled through once already, so she didn't have to be too fastidious about putting everything back in precisely the same place.

She finally made her way to the draft table. Even though the body had been moved, the dark stain on the hardwood left little doubt that this was where Pullman's body was found. Another puff from her saltcaster distributed a fine cloud of white on the floor. It wasn't long until the blown salt landed and shook itself into two distinct patterns—one the same as she'd pulled off of Pullman's journal and the other completely different.

"Huh," Martinez huffed. She crouched down and snapped a picture on her phone. Once she insured the photo matched what she saw, she kicked the salt with her foot. To her surprise, the grains deposited into four rows etched into the floor.

Martinez ran her gloved fingers over the shallow ruts that were invisible to her until they were highlighted in white. They started beside the draft table, just under the dressmaker's mannequin. She followed their progress by touch until they ended at one of the windows.

Martinez pointed her beam to the dummy; it was vintage with metal supports, not one of the lighter modern models made of fiberglass. She braced herself and tested its weight—maybe fifty or so pounds. She snapped another picture and moved on in her sweep. Although the apartment was large, its allocation of space made the search go by quickly. She probed it with her will and found nothing untoward.

Martinez performed a quick sweep of the kitchen and found the typical herbs and spices of the modern granola practitioner. She briefly paused to admire the garlic plait hanging on the wall before heading into the bathroom, where she salted the tiled floor. For magicians who didn't have the luxury of having a dedicated ritual space, the flat smooth surface of ceramic tile would do in a pinch. The blown salt stayed still, and Martinez moved on.

Pullman's bedroom was spacious, large enough to fit a king-sized bed with a nightstand on each side. The uneven wear and clutter was indicative of a single occupant, and a quick peek in the drawers revealed a nice vibrator but no condoms. The walls were bare except for a Detroit Derby Girls poster—the silhouette of a female skater in tube socks perched inside a martini glass. With her hair in a ponytail and no particular emphasis on her tits and ass, it was a pin-up turned on its head.

She set out salting, starting with the closet. Stashed on the shelf above the rod was a metal box, lead by the look and weight of it. Inside was all the standard gear of a practitioner: candles, matches, chalk, brick dust, sand, and what looked like a gris gris bag in the making. Martinez continued her search for completion, and once she was certain she hadn't missed a removable brick, a hidden panel, or loose floorboard, she slipped out of the loft and locked the door on the way out. She mulled over Caroline Holt's account and what she found at the crime scene on the drive home. Clearly, the life and death of Sarah Pullman was of interest to the Salt Mine.

It was well past midnight when Martinez made it home, and she heard voices from the kitchen. From the sounds of it, all her housemates were up. "Olly olly oxen free!" she called out once she was certain she wouldn't wake anyone up. She dropped her bag of gear and joined them in the kitchen.

Stigma was having a warm cup of something, chatting to the spectral trio dressed in nineteenth-century garb. Millie was darning a sock, Wolfhard was having a smoke, and the little girl who never spoke was playing with her dolly. "Oh good, you're safe," Wolfhard voiced his relief. Martinez was far from the first Salt Mine agent who'd lived in the house, but she was the first female one, and the Quakers had taken a shine to her.

"Of course," Martinez replied. "What do I always say?"

"Things that go bump in the night should be afraid of you," Millie answered by rote. "But that doesn't mean we don't worry," she added.

Martinez let her appreciation be known. It was nice to have someone worry about you when they didn't really have any say over your comings and goings. "You didn't need to wait up," she addressed Stigma.

He shrugged nonchalantly. "Auto-streaming got the better of me, and then the little one found me and wanted to hear a story." The translucent girl smiled at the mention of herself.

"As much as I'd love one of your stories, I'm bushed and I still have a few things to wrap up," Martinez excused herself. "Good night, all."

A round of good nights chimed behind her as she headed to the basement and pulled the hidden latch to the ritual room. In the center of the slate slab was the cooler she had pulled out of the back of her trunk. She popped the top and verified that the journal was still inside, wrapped in plastic and packed with salt. Until the booby trap was neutralized, she hadn't done anything more than check for a magical signature. Now that this was looking more like a case, her curiosity was heightened. "I wonder what's inside of you…?"

She shut everything up again and stifled a yawn on the stairs up. Martinez smiled as she heard the muffled rise and fall of Stigma's voice; from the sound of it, he was working his way to the story's climax. She was certain his ghostly audience was thrilled beyond measure, like children begging for one more story before bed.

She reached her room and turned on the light. Everything was as she'd left it. Despite her tiredness, she methodically stowed her gear; a place for everything and everything in its place. She miraculously resisted the call of her bed and instead pulled out her phone. She sent off the two magical signatures for identification and asked the analysts to start digs on Sarah Pullman and Caroline Holt—the sooner her requests were entered, the higher up on they were on the queue. Only then did Martinez undress and drift off to sleep.

Chapter Seven

Detroit, Michigan, USA
25th of September, 10:00 a.m. (GMT-4)

Detective Jennifer Cerova held the phone to her ear and nodded while she jotted down an address. "And that's 6:00 p.m. tonight?" she verified. "Perfect. Thanks a million." She placed the receiver back in the cradle and went to pour herself another cup of coffee. It wasn't nearly as nice as her first cup from home, but it was free and hot.

"Got a break?" Collins asked without looking up from his computer.

"Maybe. Sarah Pullman's derby team is practicing tonight and I tracked down the rink, which was surprisingly difficult to find out. I was planning on shaking some trees and seeing what fell out," she answered before sipping her slightly burnt coffee. She added another spoonful of sugar and tried it again—drinkable. "How are things on your end?"

Collins's grunt answered her question in brief. "The ex is a bust. Happily married and moved out of state after the wedding in June. Lives in Texas now and was definitely in the Lone Star State during our window for time of death. I stopped by her work yesterday and interviewed her boss and coworkers, looked through her workstation, and came up with nothing promising. They didn't even know she was in derby."

Cerova took a seat at her desk opposite his. "I didn't fare much better. The landlord has a copy of the keys, and there is no management company or on-site maintenance with access. No recent repairs or service requests were done on her apartment in the past six months. I still have to check out the landlord's alibi, but I'm not holding out hope. Forensics hasn't found anything on the murder weapon except the victim's own fingerprints, but they are still processing what they bagged at the scene."

"Any chance she stabbed herself?" he joked darkly.

Cerova smirked and continued, "I notified her parents, and they were naturally anxious for us to release the body. As far as they knew, Sarah wasn't seeing anyone, work was going well, and she was crushing derby. They described her as quiet and sensitive by nature, but she was 'really coming into her own' after her divorce—they were not fans of her ex."

"Do you think they are reliable historians?" he euphemized.

Cerova gave up on her miserable coffee and leaned back in her chair. She consulted her gut. "I think they're on the level. They were genuinely in shock by the news, and I didn't get the feeling they were hiding anything or whitewashing. Is it possible they didn't really know their daughter and she was just giving them the same spiel all adult kids tell their parents? Meh."

He shook his finger in the general direction of his screen. "The ME's report just came in if you want to take a gander."

Cerova logged in and hit her e-mail. Bolded lines of unread items popped up, even though she had cleared her inbox first thing this morning. She scrolled down until she saw Knoll, Douglas. "What's this?" she piped up after a minute of reading. "Postmortem bruising on the back of the neck."

Collins scanned the report on his monitor. "Struck from behind?" Collins guessed.

Cerova had spent the better part of last night combing through Pullman's social media presence and had the beginning of a hunch. She sifted through a stack of photos and put down one after another on Collins's desk. The first was Pullman's profile picture from online. The next was the team picture of Motor City Rollers. The last was her lifeless body draped over the table. Cerova smiled like the cat that ate the canary. "What do you see?"

Collins glanced at the pictures. "Our victim," he answered drily. She gave him a sarcastic scowl. "This would go much faster if you just told me what you thought."

She gave him a hint. "One of these things is not like the other."

He played along and examined them closer. "Her necklace," he replied. "She's wearing it in the other pictures but it wasn't on her body."

"Exactly," Cerova applauded her partner. She leaned back

in her chair and tented her fingers and tapped them tip-to-tip, a posture Collins had come to refer to as her "Mr. Burns" pose.

"No bruising, fingerprints, or trace materials found on the front of the neck," he recited from the ME's report. "She could have simply taken it off," Collins pointed out without directly calling out her notion as premature.

"First we go back and search the apartment. If it's not there but her teammates saw her wearing it at practice, there's a good chance that somebody ripped it off her dead body," Cerova negotiated.

Collins sighed. "It's a bit of a stretch."

"It's more than we had five minutes ago," she countered.

"Okay, we'll double check her apartment, but I'm driving and if we find it in her jewelry box or by the sink, you're buying me lunch." He gathered his coat and keys.

Cerova grabbed her kit and followed his lead. "And if we don't find it?"

"Then you get to gloat." He held the precinct door open for her.

Cerova smiled. "Collins, you and I both know I was already going to do that."

*****

Martinez's day had started off much the same as any other—a 6:00 a.m. alarm, morning calisthenics, and a quick commute to work. Pullman's journal cleared the scanner, and with clearance from the fourth floor, it was safely delivered to Chloe and Dot. If anyone could disarm the magical trap, it was the librarians. The bulk of her morning was spent reviewing her in-basket over breakfast, a protein shake of her own devising. Two of her four outstanding reimbursement requests had been approved, and the beaten manila folder containing the dailies was waiting for her as usual. She hadn't heard back on the magical signatures yet, but the analysts had already compiled background information on Caroline Holt and Sarah Pullman.

She was somewhere in the middle of Sarah Pullman's bio when the red light of the intercom blinked and buzzed on the corner of her desk. She pressed the button to open the line. "This is Lancer."

"Good morning, Lancer," David LaSalle's polished voice came over the speaker. "Leader requests an audience with you."

"Sure," she agreed breezily. "When?"

"Immediately," he answered curtly. He wasn't one to mince words.

Martinez put down her reading and grabbed her phone. "I'll be there in a few minutes."

The line went dead, and Martinez grabbed her suit jacket before leaving her office. There wasn't a strict dress code at the Salt Mine, but Martinez preferred to err on the side of overdressed. It was a sort of armor she had become accustomed to during her time at the Bureau.

When she arrived on the fourth floor, she made a beeline to LaSalle's desk. As Leader's private-secretary-slash-bodyguard, no one got to her without going through him. As soon as she saw the door to Leader's office was closed, she spoke low and out of the corner of her mouth, "Am I in trouble?" Being called to Leader's office was a happening, and it stirred something primal in her gut, like when your mother called you by your full name.

He raised an eyebrow. "Did you do anything wrong?"

In an uncharacteristically flamboyant gesture, Martinez threw her hands up. "Come on, man. Throw me a line!"

LaSalle cracked a smile and rose from behind his desk. "You'll survive." He was a tall drink of water with a broad frame and muscles that couldn't be obscured by his suit. Martinez had him pegged as Special Forces, but she didn't know for sure. For all their cordial interactions and banter, she could count on her fingers the number of things she knew about him. She couldn't even nail down his age because "black don't crack." LaSalle knew how to do his job and keep his lip buttoned. She expected nothing less for someone who served Leader, but that didn't stop her from trying.

He ushered her into Leader's office; Leader was waiting for her with a folder open on her desk. "Thank you, David. That will be all." The door closed on the austere office, and Martinez took a seat opposite the petite woman with the salt-and-pepper hair. The fleece sweater vest atop her long-sleeved flannel shirt and blue jeans screamed maple syrup farmer from Vermont, but her piercing gray eyes rectified any notion that Leader was tapping trees and cooking sap.

"Lancer, thank you for coming so quickly. I'd like to know more about what prompted the requests you put in last night," Leader jumped straight in.

Martinez cleared her throat and started talking: the call from Aloysius Hardwick, the meeting with Caroline Holt, and the investigation of Sarah Pullman's apartment. She tried to be focused and concise, but her internal critic kept chiming in. *Does my voice really sound like that? I know I didn't just say "wacked out" to Leader... Oh my god, am I still talking?*

"I wanted to make sure there was something for Salt Mine to investigate before using my FBI credentials to liaison with Detroit PD, so I put in the requests, both on the magical signatures and basic backgrounds on Holt and Pullman," Martinez concluded. When her voice trailed off, the room went silent. Leader swiveled her chair around to ponder all the pieces, and Martinez wasn't sure which was worse: feeling the weight of Leader's hawkish gaze or having no facial cues to interpret at all.

"And Chloe and Dot have this book?" Leader's crisp voice cut through the quiet.

"I gave it to them first thing this morning," Martinez affirmed.

Leader exhaled heavily as she turned her chair back

around—she was done with her thinking and a decision had been made. She pushed a folder across the desk to Martinez. "The system found a match for one of the signatures: Samuel Johnson. He had a colorful youth, but he's kept a low profile for over three decades."

Martinez started flipping through the file at Leader's instigation. Based on the clothing and haircut, the photo was quite old, but the man in the picture was handsome—a chiseled jaw, a cocky grin, and mischievous eyes. "Our interest in Mr. Johnson's involvement is twofold. First, he is a Mason, who are generally harmless except when you have a Mason who knows how to practice magic. Theoretically, they could uncover some unknown use for all that sacred geometry and alchemy." Martinez thought she heard a hint of derision from her generally unflappable boss.

"Our second concern is that Mr. Johnson has been a resident of a retirement community for the past five years. Two years ago, he moved into the assisted living section after a hip fracture and never left skilled nursing. Earlier this year, he was moved to the secure dementia wing. If he is using magic in an altered mental state, that would be worrisome, especially if it resulted in Ms. Pullman's untimely death."

Martinez flipped through the file until she found Johnson's date of birth and did the math: he turned seventy-three in March. "Can people with dementia even work magic anymore? It takes a lot of concentration and focus."

"I wouldn't think so in the later stages," Leader concurred. "But in the early stages? Possibly. Dementia starts with short-term memory loss, but the older memories often remain for much longer. They may not remember what they had for breakfast this morning, but they could tell you all about August 15, 1979. In time, there is general erosion of basic cognitive skills like mathematics and spelling, with eventual loss of executive function like reasoning and judgment. But the things with the most neural connections in the brain stick the longest, so there is no telling how long someone with dementia retains mastered skills, especially ones that go back to their youth."

Leader ended her unusually verbose exposition to assess her newest agent's readiness before issuing her instructions. "Investigate the situation and if Johnson is unstable and using magic, he will need to be eliminated discreetly."

Martinez understood and simply nodded. "And what about the death of Sarah Pullman and her mysterious journal?"

Leader weighed it briefly before answering, "Leave it with Detroit PD unless their investigation interferes with your exploration of Johnson. Let's give the twins some time with this book to see if there is something that ties her to Mr. Johnson.

"Incidentally, there is no Sarah Pullman registered as a magician in our records nor does this second signature match any in the database. You'll have to independently verify that signature is hers and follow the protocol for unregistered magicians."

Martinez buried her sarcasm but the little voice in her head couldn't help itself—*two cases for the price of one!* "Sounds good. Is there anything else before I get to work?"

"This has officially become a case. If you find it necessary, you are cleared to use greater resources. I'll have David expedite any outstanding expense reports so you are at full strength."

Based on Leader's perfunctory tone and wandering interest to the next file on top of the stack, Martinez surmised she was done. She grabbed the folder on Johnson and rose to leave. "Thank you, Leader. Have a good day."

Martinez was almost out the door when Leader spoke again, "Good work, Lancer. It would have taken many more incidents for the analysts to pick up a pattern on something like this."

"Just doing the job," she coolly answered before she crossed the threshold and closed the door behind her. Once there was a physical barrier between her and her daunting employer, Martinez could breathe freely and couldn't suppress the Cheshire grin spreading over her face.

LaSalle was typing away at his keyboard, eyes glued to the screen. Martinez composed herself and made her way to the elevator. Just as she was about pass his desk, his crisp tenor voice taunted her in a schoolyard inflection, "I told you you'd survive."

Chapter Eight

Detroit, Michigan, USA
25th of September, 3:55 p.m. (GMT-4)

Martinez didn't have to look hard to find the Masonic Temple. It was less than a mile from her house, and the giant gothic tower soared two hundred and ten feet into the air, looming over the elms of all five acres of Cass Park. It was the heart of Cass Corridor, the historic Midtown real estate that seemed to be in the perpetual process of gentrification and revitalization.

As Martinez got closer, the whole of the structure came into view: the sixteen-storied ritual tower, the less-tall Shriners International building in the back, and the modest seven-story auditorium that connected the two. The narrow arches and stark lines of the weathered limestone gave it an imposing demeanor—this was a place where serious people did serious things.

In a departure from freemason tradition, its architect built it in the neo-gothic style, and by hook and by crook, construction was completed in 1926. When it opened, it wasn't the biggest Masonic temple of its day—that distinction was only bestowed upon it after the demolition of the Chicago

Masonic Temple in 1939. Visiting the temple to investigate the roller derby drill hall was already on Martinez's schedule before Leader had made this a case, but the fact that Samuel Johnson was a member of one of the twenty-six blue lodges housed at the temple was too coincidental for her liking. Not that she would be granted access to anything private in the tower on this visit.

Martinez had been inside once before not long after she'd moved to Detroit. She'd taken a grand tour that showcased the various public rooms in all of their splendor. The care and craftsmanship were evident, but there was something gauche about trying to cram the breadth of hundreds of years of tradition from the old world into one building, one room at a time. At the time, Martinez was merely another tourist, one looking for distraction on a miserably wet Sunday. Now, she was on a case and she wondered how it would look to her more-experienced eyes.

Martinez parked her car in the lot behind the massive building and made her way to the auditorium, the only portion of the temple complex that was available to the public. She passed through the turnstile and entered the marble foyer. The majestic chandelier drew her eye to the balcony and then to the vaulted ceiling.

As she returned back to the ground, she saw the brass plaque of the iconic square and compass was set into the floor, the most recognizable sign of the Freemasons. Red velvet ropes cordoned it off from the rest of the room. Waiting to one side stood a slim woman in a pencil skirt and matching jacket. Her horned glasses were low on her nose as she reviewed the contents of the leather folder in her hands.

Martinez approached her, footsteps echoing on the alternating black and white tiles. "Ms. Clark?" she inquired.

The woman looked up and gave her a broad smile. "You must be Ms. Marvel."

"Of Discretion Minerals. And please, call me Tessa," she replied, offering the woman her card and outstretched hand. "I'm so glad you could squeeze me in today."

Clark closed her folder and gave her a firm shake before pushing up her glasses. "No problem at all. It was a stroke of luck on your part that I had a last minute cancellation. Now, I understand you were interested in one of the ballrooms for a corporate event?"

"Yes, I've been put in charge of organizing my company's Winter Gala," Martinez responded matter-of-factly.

Clark's face darkened. "This year?"

"Goodness, no! Next year's. I know The Masonic books fast and early," Martinez cheerfully answered.

Clark nodded approvingly at her preparedness. "You were wise to do so. Shall we proceed?"

Martinez smiled. "Lead the way." Clark proceeded down the stairs to a vast circular room with pillars interspersed throughout. Her guide flipped a series of switches on a panel and bright white light flooded the room from the recessed fixtures in the ceiling.

"This is the Fountain Ballroom, and it can accommodate up to a thousand people, give or take a hundred. Because the space is so large, we have more flexibility in arrangements and decor. We also offer an assortment of ancillary services, including catering," she effortlessly began her sales pitch.

"Additionally, we can adjust the lighting for a more atmospheric mood." With the turn of a few knobs, the overhead lights dimmed, soft light glowed from sconces on the wall, and a pale blue emanated from the tops of pillars, spilling onto the ceiling like fountains of light. "We can also do different colors, if you like," she added.

"It's lovely but quite spacious. Do you have something a little smaller…more personal?" Martinez tactfully asked.

Clark's face remained neutral. "I understand. Perhaps the Crystal Ballroom is more of what you are looking for." She switched off the lights and descended down another half floor. She opened the doors to a long rectangular room that was classical Italian decor at its finest—clean eggshell plaster walls with ornately painted panels, a polished wooden floor, the double staircase leading to the second-story portico with rounded openings into the main room, and soft curves of the painted arches. The pièce de résistance was the intricately painted panel on the ceiling with inset half domes between two grand chandeliers.

Clark let the ambiance of the setting do the heavy lifting and allowed her perspective client to soak it all in before speaking. "This is the Crystal Ballroom. It can accommodate 550 people. The lighting can be adjusted as well."

Martinez took her time before responding to help sell her cover. "It is certainly beautiful and has that more-personal feel. But, thinking about it, perhaps I spoke too soon regarding the size of the Fountain Ballroom. These things do have a tendency to grow as the event draws near as I'm sure you know; plus ones turn into plus twos. I think it would be best if I could have information on both rooms and have the weekend to run some numbers?" Martinez requested.

"Certainly," Clark graciously replied. From her leather folder, she presented cover sheets that neatly folded into a pamphlet. "My card is inside, as well."

"Excellent." Martinez tucked it into her bag. "I wonder if I could ask you for a favor?"

Clark smiled, but her eyes turned cautious. "What can I do for you, Tessa?"

"Would I be able to take a peek at the newly renovated ceiling in the drill hall? It was still under repair when I toured in the spring, and it would be nice to see it without the hustle of all those roller skaters crashing into each other."

Clark's tension relaxed—a small request to secure a large booking. "I think that can be arranged. Let's take the elevator."

Like the brass plaque on the floor, the bronze doors of the

elevator bore the square and compasses, with a prominent G in the center. They passed the Main Theater and locker room and went straight to the top floor.

Home to Detroit Roller Derby, the drill hall had been designed for martial training. The floating, sprung floor was made to soften marchers' steps, but it was also perfect for all manner of modern athletics—including roller derby—with the added benefit of noise reduction. It had one of the largest wooden floors anywhere—large enough to fit three NBA basketball courts side-by-side.

Clark turned a switch. Gone was the dropped ceiling added in the 1980s, and in its place was the plastered ceiling and Pratt trusses of 1926, lit by the hanging chandeliers. Martinez had remembered being blown over by the size of the room on the tour, but it didn't prepare her for its transformation. The reclaimed height—twenty-nine feet at its apex—made the huge room feel even larger.

Martinez cast her will in Clark's direction. *Hail Mary, full of grace…* "Oh, it's okay if you need to use the restroom. I can wait here," she spoke blithely.

Clark blinked a few times and bashfully commented, "I do apologize."

Martinez waved her hand, nonplussed. "I'll be fine in here."

As soon as Clark left the room, Martinez went to work. She didn't have much time and the space was much too large to salt without precision—she needed answers quick. She pulled a hag stone from her pocket. It would allow her to immediately see anything magical, but staring through it for too long was dangerous. She started counting as soon as she peered through the hole. *One, two, three...* She hurriedly scanned the room.

Martinez found her objective immediately: three tangential circles nestled within the innermost oval. There was a faint blue glow to them and it seemed to vibrate under her gaze. She could feel the draw of its power through the hag stone. *Eight, nine...*she asserted her will and pulled it away from her eye before she reached the count of ten.

That was weird, she thought as she cleared her head: she hadn't seen anything resonate like that through a hag stone before. She pulled out her vape pen and hustled to the infield. With a strong puff, she cast a spray of fine salt and waited. The magical signature shook itself out—the same as on the journal and at the scene of the crime. She cast two more times, once at each circle. Assuming it belonged to Sarah Pullman, whatever she was doing in here, she did it alone.

She hurriedly snapped pictures of all the signatures, and kicked the salt to break the pattern each time she was done. She had just enough time to put away her gear before Clark returned to find Tessa Marvel, Assistant Director of Acquisitions at Discretion Minerals, staring up at the chandeliers in awe. "The space is really amazing with the renovation, although it makes the track stick out like a sore thumb."

"Oh, that won't be a problem next year," Clark reassured

her. The polished woman instantly frowned—she had no idea what possessed her to say such a thing.

Martinez streamed out a little more of her will to loosen Clark's tongue. "What do you mean?" she probed.

"We are not renewing the derby's lease on this space now that it's got such potential. This will be their last season at the Masonic Temple." Clark's demeanor completely bottomed out and Martinez dispelled her will—she had pushed Clark as far as she could without becoming draconian about it. "I don't know why I just said that. That's not common knowledge."

Martinez tilted her head to the one side. "Who am I going to tell?"

Chapter Nine

Detroit, Michigan, USA
25th of September, 6:05 p.m. (GMT-4)

Leigh Meyer ran into the rink and quickly kicked off her shoes. She was only five minutes late, but she knew how hollow that would sound to the coach. She whipped her lustrous ebony locks into a rough bun and put on her gear: knee pads, elbow pads, wrist guards, helmet, and mouth guard. She grabbed her skates, reflexively checking them before donning them: toe stop tight, bushings look good, and wheels spinning freely with just enough lateral movement to be flexible without any appreciable loss in power. Methodically, she tightened her laces from the toe up and doubled knotted them at the top.

Meyer rolled to the bar on the edge of the rink and warmed up with squats—they were a pain in the best of circumstances, but she gained a whole new appreciation for just how torturous they could be when done on quad skates. Once her hips and knees were loose, she joined the pack of skaters in their warm up, starting with scissors. Bent at the knees, Meyers pushed her legs out with her gluts and pulled them back in with her abs, crossing over on the curves. Derby was essentially a nonstop core exercise with leg day thrown in for good measure. Meyer was naturally fit and curvaceous, but there was no denying that derby had accentuated her silhouette, which didn't hurt her day job: Mistress Scarlet, professional dominatrix at 18 is 9.

She was just getting warm when the call for devil laps was given. The skaters of Motor City Rollers broke into two groups and took turns racing the rink. As a jammer, speed was essential for Meyer—scoring points by lapping the opposing team's skaters was her responsibility. Although she'd been competing for several years, she still found the name ironic: who'd think to find a real succubus doing devil laps?

At the piercing whistle, she took off with her cohort and moved to the front of the pack as she came to full speed. She reveled in the rush—it was as close as she could get to flying while still staying on earth. Not for the first time, she lamented that she couldn't skate in her true form. Her tail would have helped with balance and a good wing buffet would knock any blocker out of her way. Unfortunately, mortals tended to freak out when one went full devil.

"Scarlet, tighten up!" Coach Kent yelled from the sidelines. Meyer had gone by many names since her banishment from hell all those centuries ago, a different one for each human form she had assumed. She generally preferred taking the female form, although she had been known to adopt a male guise every so often, just to change things up. Leigh Meyer was her latest identity, but on the track, she was #142, Scarlet Leather. To her parents, she would always be Meridiana, their afflicted offspring cursed to no longer perform evil acts, a prodigal child that could never return home. Meridiana heard the call and adjusted posture: core tight, shoulders straight, chin up.

The team alternated between sprinting laps and calisthenics, the number of laps and sets increasing with each pass. Meridiana was breathing heavily and sweating by the time she finished sprinting ten laps in one go. She drank some water with the rest of her group and took in the gritty resolve of the determined women around her.

As a succubus, she didn't technically need food or drink, but much of human interaction revolved around its intake, so much so that she had become accustomed to partaking, even though it gave her no sustenance. She subsisted on psychic energy.

Back when she had been a full-fledged devil, it was simply a matter of torturing humans or eating souls when she felt peckish. It was only after being cursed that she'd come to understand that both were evil, and she had to figure out another way to nourish herself. Now, she fed on heightened emotional states, and as a seductive infiltrator, Meridiana had stuck with what she knew best: sex. The BDSM scene had deep roots, and there was no better niche for a hungry succubus that could no longer do evil.

Roller derby was a recent discovery, introduced to her by an old flame who'd dragged her to a bout. Like so many unacquainted with the sport, Meridiana had assumed it was basically burlesque on wheels with the theatrics of wrestling. She was not expecting a competitive, full-contact team sport dominated by all stripes of women. The surge of intense emotions overwhelmed her; it was like being a kid in a candy shop.

When Meridiana started training, her pride wasn't the only thing that got bruised—unsurprising, since roller skates were not essential kit for a devil. As she improved and rose in the rosters, she came to understand that although derby was different things to different skaters, everyone exuded a tremendous amount of cathartic force as they skated, toe stepped, leaped, and spun their way on the track. And then there were the body slams and takedowns—the actualization of aggression and pain that somehow wasn't malevolent. It was a different sort of energy that required a different kind of intimacy on her part, but it tasted complex and delicious. The spread was so bountiful and diverse, it was like dining at a buffet, and Meridiana could take a bite of this and that at her pleasure.

While everyone was taking five, two visitors entered the rink and approached the resting pack. Meridiana recognized them and immediately stopped grazing—a visit from homicide detectives was never a good thing. She did a quick head count and came up one short. Sadie was missing.

Tracy Kent, coach of the Motor City Rollers, held no truck with nonsense, and people interrupting her practice was definitely nonsense. She had been there from the beginning, when the women who loved derby revived it and turned it into the honest sport it was today: by the skaters, for the skaters. She was one of the founders of Detroit Roller Derby, back when it had been called Detroit Derby Girls. Even after she'd retired from competition, she wasn't done with derby. Kent remained active in the league and started coaching after ten years as a blocker. Being on this end of the whistle wasn't the same as playing, but it was gratifying in its own way. Sure, she hadn't body slammed into anyone recently, but she also hadn't broken anything, either.

Kent skated toward them and slid her back foot behind and perpendicular to her front, stopping a few feet away from them with a perfect T-stop. "Rink's closed. This is a private practice," she brusquely stated.

The two detectives both pulled out their identification, but it was Cerova that spoke first. "I'm Detective Jennifer Cerova of Detroit PD. I'm looking for the Motor City Rollers."

Kent looked at their flip wallets up close before looking up. "You've found them. I'm Tracy Kent, their coach." She extended her hand and delivered a firm shake. "What's all this about?"

"I'm here to ask you and the team some questions about the recent death of Sarah Pullman."

Kent looked confused. "Who?"

"Sarah Pullman," Cerova repeated.

"You may know her as Slashy Sadie," Collins offered when Kent made no sign of recognition.

The coach's face lit up in recognition. "Oh, Sadie! A real shame. ValKillrie told me about her passing before practice. She was one hell of a blocker. Even though she was on the small side, she could get to where you needed her to be and she had a real bead on running plays and team work."

"We were actually more interested in her comings and goings in the days preceding her death," Cerova steered back to the case. "We understand she was at practice Sunday night?"

"Yup. Took a nasty fall but got right back up again," Kent confirmed.

"Was she wearing this at practice?" Cerova held up a magnified picture of a red jade donut hanging from Pullman's neck.

Kent shrugged. "Probably. I recognize it as something she often wore, but I can't say for certain she was wearing it Sunday. You might want to ask one of the other skaters about that sort of thing."

Cerova tried a different approach. "Would you say you were close to Sadie?"

"About derby stuff? Sure. Outside of that? I can't say that I was," Kent said unapologetically. She nodded to the cluster of skaters behind her. "I'm their coach. I focus on what matters on the track: how hard they hit, how fast they get back up, and how much heart they bring to the game. I don't need to know their real names or what's going on in their personal lives." Her answer befuddled Cerova, and the detective failed to hide it.

"I know it sounds harsh, but it's really freeing for a lot of them. On the track, they aren't defined by their hardships, disappointments, or traumas. They are just athletes playing with their team. For some, it's the only time people see them for what they are capable of and not their damage," Kent explained. "Generally speaking, happy people with charmed lives don't play derby."

"I see. In that case, we'd like the opportunity to talk to her teammates one by one," Collins picked up the conversation as his partner regained her footing. Kent sized them up before eventually instructing them to follow her. Cerova and Collins exchanged looks as she skated away from them, but ultimately they obeyed.

Kent rolled back to the pack, who had regained their breath and curiosity. Their private chatter and speculation came to halt when the coach blew her whistle. She addressed her skaters. "As some of you know, Sadie passed away some time after last practice. These are detectives from Detroit PD and they would like to ask you all some questions. It's up to you if you want to speak to them, but I'd like to remind you that someone hurt one of ours and these are the people in charge of bringing them to justice." She paused to let the gravitas of the situation sink in. Cerova and Collins waited with their hands behind their backs.

Then, Kent returned to form. "That's all I'll say about that. We're going to break into stations. Jammers, pivots, and relief, set up for toe stop spins on the line, mohawks, and line toe stop shuffles. I need you nimble. Mantis, set up the cones for rolling coverage drills. If you aren't going down one of those stations, pair up for zone defense—reverse mirror and solo trapping. Then, we'll finish up with a round of kill the jammer.

A round of groans erupted, but Kent yelled over them, "They just posted the matches for the season, and we are going against Grandprix Madonnas in one month. They won't be easy on you, so neither am I." She gave three short tweets and the women dispersed.

Kent turned back around to the detectives. "Talk to whoever you want, but I've got a practice to run."

Chapter Ten

Detroit, Michigan, USA
25th of September, 6:48 p.m. (GMT-4)

Doug Knoll puttered around his office and watched the clock. Twelve more minutes and he was done for the day. He generally liked his job and found a certain freedom in plying his medical skills to solve mysterious deaths. It beat trying to convince people to take their medicine, and certainly, none of them had "done their research on the internet." But today, he hoped and prayed that should a corpse be found, it would be after the next twelve minutes, at which time it would be someone else's problem.

Just then, a knock landed on his door. One of the techs popped his head inside, "Doug, you got a visitor waiting for you up front."

"Is it the funeral home for Sarah Pullman?" Knoll asked.

"No, it's FBI. Agent Martinez?"

Knoll sat up and checked his appearance on his phone: no food in his beard or teeth, his hair wasn't sticking up, and while his shirt wasn't particularly flattering, it was clean. He checked his breath and grabbed a mint from his desk before leaving his office.

"Agent Martinez, what a pleasant surprise," he greeted her. She was still as pretty as he remembered. She was doing something different with her hair; swept away bangs softened her face and made her look more mysterious.

"Better than a new corpse, I imagine," she said dryly.

He laughed a little too loud before reining it in. "How can I help you?"

"I'm here to visit one of your occupants," she euphemized. "Is Sarah Pullman still with you?"

"Yes, but her body was released today and I was waiting for the funeral home to pick her up," he informed her.

She shifted her shoulders. "Mind if I take a quick look?"

Knoll looked at his watch before flagging her through. "If you make it fast." He led her into the cold room and retrieved Ms. Pullman from her cubby. Martinez grabbed a pair of gloves from the box on the wall and drew back the sheet. This was her first eyes on Sarah Pullman, and she hadn't read the autopsy to guide her search. Martinez would put her money on the hole in Sarah's chest was the cause of death, but she began her search in earnest nonetheless.

Knoll couldn't contain his curiosity. "What exactly are you looking for?"

"Not sure yet, but I'll know when I see it," she answered without looking up; she wanted to make sure she got what she needed before Pullman was processed at the funeral home. "Anything strike you as odd about this one?"

"Nope. Sharp pair of scissors slid between T4 and T5 right into the heart and she bled out," he responded. He could have sworn she looked crestfallen at the news. "They can't all be death by space vacuum," he joked. He grinned deeper when she let out a terse laugh.

Her face turned quizzical. "What's this?" She pointed to a three-millimeter dark spot on Pullman's shoulder.

"Junctional melanocytic nevi," he answered authoritatively. "Otherwise known as a mole."

She gave a nod and continued her scan. There was something endearing about the juxtaposition of her dogged demeanor during her methodical exam and the way she kept blowing back the errant lock of hair that drifted into her line of vision.

Knoll mustered his courage. "My shift's about to end. You wanna get some coffee?"

She moved to the last of Pullman's limbs. "It's a little late for coffee," she said neutrally.

"How about some food?" he persisted.

Martinez looked up from Pullman and pulled her gloves off like a pro—inside out, one into the other. "I don't go on dates with anyone I interact with for work."

"Who's calling it a date? We're two colleagues that haven't had dinner yet. We could discuss Pullman's autopsy over burgers. Only a crazy person would talk about corpses on a date," he said nonchalantly.

Before she could answer, a tech came through the door. "Doug, the funeral home is here for Pullman."

"Okay, I'll be right there. I just have to sign the paperwork in my office and they can take her away," he answered and shooed the tech away with a nod of his head. When they were alone again, he asked Martinez, "So, what do you think?"

She brushed her hair out of her eyes and sighed. "You go take care of your paperwork. We'll both be here when you get back."

"Great, I'll just be a minute," he affirmed as he backed out of the room, nearly knocking over a Mayo stand in the process.

Once he left the room, Martinez pocketed the gloves in which she'd collected a few strands of Pullman's hair. She pulled the sheet over Pullman and cast salt from her vape pen—it was a match. She snapped a picture on her phone. Then, she ruffled the sheet and let the salt fall to the ground. The spot on Pullman's right shoulder revealed and concealed itself as the white sheet rose and fell. On a hunch, Martinez exchanged her vape pen for the hag stone and discovered that it was as she suspected—it wasn't just a mole.

*****

"I'm home," Martinez called out to her living and ghostly housemates as she entered the house and closed the door behind her.

Stigma muted the TV. "Did you have fun with the doctor?" he called from the couch.

She locked the keyless deadbolt and shed her gear on the table tucked under the stairs. "We had burgers and talked about a corpse," she answered ambivalently.

"I've had worse dates," he offhandedly remarked.

"It wasn't a date. I was very clear on that from the beginning," she insisted as she kicked off her shoes. "I wasn't even going to go, but by not immediately saying no, I got more time alone with the corpse without having to break into the funeral home later tonight. By the time he returned, it was just easier to go." She joined Stigma on the couch and watched a very lean but very strong Japanese man on the TV hike a bar up a salmon ladder. "That is just bonkers."

"I know, right? Still, it's inspiring," he commented, tactfully letting it slide that she could have easily magicked her way out of it if she really didn't want to go. Instead, he chose to elucidate his point using the Socratic method. "Did you pay for your food?"

"Of course."

"Did he offer to pay but you turned him down?"

Martinez brushed her hair aside. "Yes," she admitted.

"Did he call you Teresa or Agent Martinez?"

She closed one eye and tried to remember. "Both."

"I know you didn't give him anything," Stigma qualified, "but did he dig for personal information or tell you about himself in a tit-for-tat maneuver."

Martinez squinched her face. "That's not really a fair question. He's a really gregarious guy, and he can't help but overshare." Stigma looked askance but said nothing.

"Last question: did he try to engage physical contact before you parted ways?"

"I shook his hand," she said emphatically.

"That wasn't the question," he singsonged.

"I stuck out my hand when it looked like he was coming in close," she confessed.

"It was totally a date," Stigma declared his verdict. "A disastrous one for him, but time will tell if he's a glass-half-full kind of guy."

"Hopefully another ME will do the next couple of autopsies I need in Wayne County," Martinez said wistfully and changed the subject. "On to more important topics, what do you know about witches' marks?"

"As in the excuse pervy religious men used to strip-search women during witch hunts?"

"Yeah, except this one is on my dead, unregistered magician."

Stigma whistled. "Any sign of a devil?"

"Nope. Not in her apartment, on her corpse, or where she was doing her casting." Her body sank deeper into the cushions as the fatigue of the day finally caught up with her.

"Sounds like something to ask Chloe and Dot," he

concluded and turned the sound back on. The cheers of the crowd returned as the contestant finished the course and Martinez tapped away on her phone.

Chapter Eleven

Detroit, Michigan, USA
25th of September, 9:35 p.m. (GMT-4)

Meridiana stepped out of the steamy bathroom, enrobed in soft, fluffy terrycloth. She didn't have much time to spare but insisted on showering before work. She was always drenched after a grueling derby practice, and she refused to leather up before cleaning up. Plus, the heat and steam helped her think.

Meridiana rubbed her long black locks in the towel, absorbing as much moisture as possible before she pulled out her blow dryer. She snapped on the diffuser, gently drying her scalp before switching to the concentrator and roller brush. As she methodically worked each section, her mind wandered in the drone of the hairdryer. The more Meridiana thought about it, the more it rubbed her wrong. She didn't like that two female magicians within her social sphere had been killed so close together. People died all the time, but their proximity to her made her suspicious. Was someone or something targeting her?

She had centuries of dodging interaction with the police, but in the past six weeks, she had been interviewed twice by homicide detectives. Usually, this kind of attention would make her contemplate bailing and picking a different form, but changing identities was such a pain. More than just the upheaval of breaking off and starting over as someone new, she *liked* being Leigh Meyer. Meyer had a rewarding job and hobby that kept her well fed and engaged. Between them, Meyer had found a community of sorts. She almost felt human.

Seated at her vanity, Meridiana began moisturizing her body before getting dressed, starting with her facial cream and working down her body. She warmed the lotion in her hands before applying it to her creamy skin—yes, she very much liked this form. The tender spot on her left hip smarted at her touch. She had landed hard when Kissmet body slammed her, only because she was going so fast from the hip whip she took off Lessie Borden.

The skin was just started to discolor. *Well, that's not going to do*, Meridiana tutted. She weaved her will, and the purples and reds faded until her skin was unmarred. She smiled at her handiwork. Luckily, vanity was not evil.

She pulled out a tight sweater, a short skirt, and harlequin cotton leggings—the evenings were getting cold, but that was no reason to skimp on looking fashionable. She considered her options while she dressed. She couldn't ask her mother—they had just spoken a month ago and she would become suspicious if Meridiana called so soon after their last conversation. She wasn't on great terms with any of her siblings; they only reached out to her when they were rebelling or already in trouble.

Devils were a very ordered community by nature, and much of their efforts were spent climbing up the hierarchy, usually through trading favors, shifting alliances, and pushing someone else further down. She was frankly dumbfounded there hadn't been more upset in the seats of power with her father out of hell for so long, but his shadow had always been long and dark.

Once she could no longer trade in the currency of the litigious and treacherous fiends, Meridiana lost a lot of social capital, something she was surprised to discover she didn't really miss. After her affliction—as her mother euphemistically referred to it— she was no longer a target for ambitious devils. She enjoyed the unexpected freedom of her demotion. She liked not having to constantly anticipate the next betrayal. But now she was wondering if lax conditions had left her flat-footed.

She slid on knee-high boots one at a time and faced hard facts—she was short on leverage and even shorter on allies, which meant she had to make the most of what she had. She grabbed her work bag, stuffed with all sorts of toys and her favorite corset. She was out the door when her phone buzzed in her hand. ValKillrie had sent out a mass message to the team: tomorrow evening was visiting hours for Slashy Sadie, aka Sarah Pullman, followed by an address and time.

Normally, Meridiana would have deleted the message and thought nothing more about it. They weren't particularly close, and she had better things to do than mark a mortal's death in solemn ceremony. But this time, she merely tucked her phone away and got in her car. Perhaps she could find answers her own way.

Although Meridiana was exiled from Hell and cursed to do no evil, she wasn't without her powers, just limited in *how* she could use them. She still had the will and ability, but if it was evil, things simply wouldn't work. It had taken her some time to figure out what constituted as evil; unsurprisingly, the question of morality never came up when she was employed as a succubus.

The most confounding aspect for Meridiana was how much context played a role in the determination. Sure, some acts were inherently evil and therefore off-limits. Take, for example, eating souls. If there was a way to eat a mortal's soul and have it *not* be evil, she hadn't found it. And it wasn't from a lack of trying. But there was a much larger field of acts that weren't intrinsically evil but could be given the circumstances. As they said, the devil was in the details.

Back when she was used as an infiltrator, she had to ability to see through a mortal's eyes—sometimes literally, if she needed specific information, sometimes metaphorically if she needed to understand which buttons to push to steer her target in the right direction. It was the equivalent of eavesdropping on memories, which came in handy as a succubus. When her lovers feel asleep postcoitally, she had the run of their memories. She had done it a million times and it never crossed her mind that it could be evil until the first time—post curse—she'd tried it and it didn't work.

At the time, she frustratingly added "rifling through someone's innermost thoughts and memories without their knowledge" to her evil list and moved on. Now, however, as she drove to 18 is 9, she thought she could make an argument that it's not evil if the person is dead and it's done in an attempt to find the killer. She gave it serious thought while she parked and got ready in her dressing room. By the time she had pinned up her hair and laced up her corset, she had come to a decision.

There was only way to find out, and she always looked good in black.

Chapter Twelve

Detroit, Michigan, USA
26th of September, 1:05 p.m. (GMT-4)

Martinez wound her way through the crystalline halls of the sixth floor past the stacks toward the circular reference desk of Chloe and Dot. She was looking for the librarians, and finding them was always a gamble—as conjoined twins, when you found one, you found both, but it was always all or nothing.

This afternoon, Martinez was in luck. Chloe and Dot sat with their dirty blonde heads bent down, intently reading, each with a cup of coffee. "Anybody want to pumpkin spice that?" she greeted them with a bottle of flavored creamer—it never hurt to bring the librarians a treat from time to time.

Chloe looked up first with a cheerful smile. "Yes, please and thank you!"

"It's not even October," Dot said with mild disdain without stopping her reading.

Chloe shrugged as she shook the bottle. "That's fine; more for me." A spicy aroma erupted as she popped the seal and mingled with the smell of all those books.

"I didn't say I didn't want any," Dot remarked as she slid

her mug toward her sister.

Martinez smiled at their banter and jabs and took it as a positive sign that all was right with the world. If the twins weren't bickering, it meant they had bigger things to worry about. "Did you get a look at the picture I sent last night?"

Chloe savored her first sip before answering. "The witches' mark? Yeah, there are a couple of situations in which a person can acquire it, including making a pact with a devil."

"Wait, that's real?" Martinez interrupted her.

"Sure, but it's much more rare that the witch trials made it out to be. To people that aren't magicians, they are indistinguishable to moles. But you didn't find a fiendish signature?"

"Nope," Martinez confirmed.

"So, it's more likely that she was born with it. Some old families pass along their magical aptitude, along with the mark, through the maternal line."

"So there is a good chance that Sarah Pullman's mother is a magician," Martinez reasoned.

"Not necessarily," Dot piped up after sipping her coffee and grunting for more creamer —for someone so dark, she liked her coffee sweet and creamy. Chloe obliged. "It's more like a boon, but it doesn't mean you have to practice the craft."

Martinez hemmed and hawed. "So it looks like I need to talk to Sarah Pullman's mother."

"Wouldn't be a bad idea if you want to figure out what

she was doing. Mothers have a way of knowing things when it comes to their kids." Chloe darted her eyes to Dot.   "Worst part of being a conjoined twin? Feeling pain when your sister is getting punished for doing something wrong." Dot grinned behind her coffee.

"Any progress on the journal I dropped off yesterday?" Martinez kept them on topic.

"Yup. It's over there." Chloe pointed to one side of the circular desk. "The book itself isn't magical but the booby trap was. It's a good thing you didn't try to read it. It's safe now if you want to see what's inside."

"Spoiler alert: it's super boring," Dot interjected.

Martinez picked up the notebook and started flipping. "How did you get rid of the booby trap?"

"Old family trick. We made a purification circle with baking soda instead of chalk. Of course, in the old days, you couldn't buy it by the box for less than a dollar. They had to refine minerals for soda ash."

"Baking soda? Huh, not just for raising baked goods and deodorizing," Martinez made conversation as she perused the pages. Dot wasn't wrong—Pullman's journal was basically a collection of sketches and doodles with some random columns of numbers. Without context, it was hard to imagine anything in here was important enough to warrant a magical padlock, much less get stabbed over.

"You ever notice that when people doodle, they draw the

same thing over and over again. Maybe not exactly the same, but generally variations on a theme. It's what their hands are doing while their minds are otherwise preoccupied," Martinez observed as she skimmed.

"Is this going somewhere?" Dot finally picked her head up from her book.

"Yes," Martinez said pointedly. "Sarah Pullman kept drawing ovals in the corners and margins, and I'm assuming the larger ones with Xs and Os are plays for derby. But more importantly, I've seen this one in real life." She laid the journal open and turned it around so the twins could see. It was three circles lined up in a row inside an oval. The circles touched each other as well as the oval. "That's what Sarah Pullman put in place at the drill hall in the Masonic Temple. Any idea what it is?"

"Masons!" Dot muttered derisively.

"What Dot means to say is that we concern ourselves with real magic, not a bunch of men dressing up in regalia with secret handshakes in their boy's club," Chloe translated. "But we do have some masonic literature under fiction." Dot smirked at that.

"What I saw was real magic," Martinez reassured them. "It was blue and electric through the hag stone, and Sarah Pullman's signature was all over it."

Chloe and Dot both stopped their snickering. "Did you touch it?"

"No, but I got the feeling it wanted me to," Martinez replied. The librarians got off their chairs in unison and went to the stacks. "Should I be following you?"

"Stay put. You'll only slow us down," Dot called back.

Martinez kept flipping and found pages of equations with portions scratched out and corrected until they were rewritten in their latest incarnation, only to be given the same treatment. There were other shapes with notions and numbers with a Greek letter sprinkled every so often. She knew they were used in higher-level mathematics but couldn't recall their precise meaning or use.

When they returned to the desk, Dot was flipping through a book with "Sacred Geometry" on the spine while Chloe took the journal from Martinez's hands. They put them side-by-side, cackling with glee.

"She did it. She found the golden circle!" Chloe exclaimed. "Who would have thought it was an ellipse?"

"All it took was a woman to find it," Dot sniped.

"Golden circle?" Martinez spoke up.

Chloe gave her the quick and dirty. "The Masons are what happens when religion, science, and mathematics have a mutant love child. They were big on the alchemy thing, trying to find the right formula to change various metals into gold. They were also obsessed with looking for the perfect mathematical things, which were then dubbed 'golden.'"

"They basically circle-jerked to Pythagoras for figuring out the $a^2+b^2=c^2$ because that gave them the golden ratio, which led them to the golden rectangle, the golden proportion, the golden section, the golden mean—" Dot rattled off.

"I get it. They were really into gold," Martinez cut her short. "I'm sure these ideas were groundbreaking in their day, but now, it looks like what I was doing in my eighth grade geometry class with compasses and all those funny rulers."

"Which is why practitioners generally scoff at Masons," Chloe explained. "The Masons thought they could create magical effects through super symmetry—harnessing the unseen power and all that. Magicians knew differently."

"But we use circles all the time!" Martinez objected.

"To limit magic," Chloe clarified. "Summoning circles, protection circles, entering the Magh Meall—they are all designed as lines of demarcation. On this side, magic; on the other side, no magic."

"So what happens when a magician uses masonic principles and powers it with actual magic?" Martinez asked.

"That's theoretically impossible. It's like mixing water and oil—they naturally separate. Magic isn't logical, and geometry is. Geometry is just logic brought into the physical dimensions," Dot answered.

"So you're saying that my unregistered magician with a witches' mark found a way to make a magic-Mason emulsion?" Martinez mixed her metaphors. What she lacked in mathematics, she made up in her prowess in the kitchen.

"It looks like it. Can we keep this? We may be able to work through some of these equations with Weber and figure out what they mean," Chloe requested as a formality, but the journal was already clutched in her hands.

Martinez knew better than to refuse the librarians access to a book. "Sure. I'm headed up to my office for a bit. Let me know when you come up with something."

Chloe had already picked up the receiver to phone Weber. "Will do. Thanks for the creamer," she called out while Dot was taking a closer look at the equations and columns of numbers.

It was a short elevator ride to the fifth floor, and Martinez held her palm to the scanner outside her office. While she waited for the door to unlock, she looked across to Wilson's office and wondered what happened when an agent didn't come back. How did they get inside and reset the doors? For that matter, how did the dailies get there every morning? Did Wilson have stacks of beaten manila folders waiting for him if and when he returned?

She ended her rambling thoughts once she heard the audible click and went inside—sometimes it was better not to ask. She switched the lights on and unloaded her gear. She had spent the morning working out of the office, using the FBI database and the internet to supplement what the Salt Mine had given her. It was one of the things she didn't like about her job: going into the office meant being cut off from the internet. Everything was connected to the internet, and while Martinez understood the inverse relationship between ease of access and security, sometimes it made it harder to do her job. In that way, being out in the field was nice. She could have remote backup from the analysts and the librarians without giving up connectivity.

But there were things she could not do remotely, like enter Sarah Pullman into the Salt Mine records posthumously. Now that she had verified her unique magical signature at the morgue, it was time to make her official, witches' mark and all. Martinez waited for her computer to boot up, contemplating what to do about the other magician in this case: Samuel Johnson.

She had read over his Salt Mine file yesterday. Apart from some arrests protesting the Vietnam War, he didn't have a criminal record. He landed on the Salt Mine's radar for some indiscreet magic use during said protests, and he was cautioned and let off with a warning. They hadn't had any problems from him in decades. He'd worked on some of the most beloved children's programs of the '70s and '80s as a skilled puppeteer before eventually getting married and settling in Ann Arbor where he operated a children's theater until he retired.

He'd joined the Masons around that time—the same lodge as his father-in-law, so it wasn't hard to piece together how that happened. His wife passed away five years ago, and two months after her death, he moved into Evergreen Meadows. Again, nothing out of the ordinary there. Besides being a Mason that could practice the arts, there wasn't anything that stood out as unusual, except that his signature was found in a murdered magician's apartment.

Yesterday afternoon she'd put in a request, but the analysts hadn't found any connection between him and Pullman. If they couldn't find one, there was a good chance it didn't exist. On paper, they were perfect strangers; but Martinez knew when it came to magic, connections were not always so apparent.

Which led her to her real problem: access to Samuel Johnson. If he were wandering Detroit freely, she would have her choice of how to conduct surveillance, assessment, and resolution. Unfortunately, he was an Alzheimer's patient in a locked unit, and if it was anything like the place her grandfather had been in, Johnson wouldn't even be able to get out of the ward without punching in a code at the door.

Additionally, her normal aliases were useless. Martinez had scoped out Evergreen Meadows yesterday, and it was the elderly equivalent of a lifestyle apartment. It was the kind of place that had protocols for everything, and showing a badge would start a cascade of attention Martinez would rather avoid. As a vulnerable person, it was the facility's responsibility to keep him safe and protect his rights, which included being questioned by the FBI. Even if she was given an audience, it wouldn't be one-on-one.

That's why she requested a different dig this morning— this one into Samuel Johnson's family. Whenever someone moved into one of these senior communities, there was a slew of paperwork: list of kin, emergency contacts, and advanced directives or a living will at the very minimum. Samuel Johnson didn't have any kids and his parents were long dead. Unless he was entirely alone in the world, someone would have to be listed to make decisions on his behalf should he become incapacitated, or at the very least be notified if something happened to him. There was a good chance that person was a relative, and that might provide a way in.

The operating system came on screen, and she returned her sights to Sarah Pullman. Martinez plodded away at filling in the required cells as the entirety of Pullman's thirty-seven years unfolded: family, residence, education, employment, magical signature, and known esoteric activity. As always, there was a place for narrative input—the things about a person that don't easily fit in a category or field.

Martinez typed in her involvement in Detroit Roller Derby and connection to the Masonic Temple. She entered the particulars of her death and the things that had come to light since Caroline Holt had given Martinez Pullman's journal. She uploaded the pertinent supporting pictures to the file and clicked save. Martinez knew she wasn't done with Sarah Pullman's profile by a long shot.

Martinez looked at her watch and planned the rest of the afternoon accordingly. Pullman's visitation started at 6:00 p.m., and if she wanted a private moment with her mother, she couldn't be late.

Chapter Thirteen

Detroit, Michigan, USA
26th of September, 5:47 p.m. (GMT-4)

Detective Cerova pulled into a distant parking spot at Plymouth Funeral Home. Although she technically could attend the visitation, families did not take kindly to the police showing up, even if it was in pursuit of finding whoever was responsible for the death of their loved one. It was a time for grieving, not interrogation, and if the perpetrator wasn't caught, this could be the only closure they would get.

Cerova respected the family's wishes, but that didn't mean she couldn't observe from the outside: who came in and out, and what they did when they thought no one was watching. She cracked the windows before cutting the engine and settled in for a long watch. Her thermos and binoculars were on the passenger seat, as well as a sandwich in case she got hungry.

She'd really thought she had something when she and Collins searched Pullman's apartment and came up short one necklace. Multiple teammates confirmed that Pullman was wearing it at practice Sunday night, even if they were lacking in other insight.

Unfortunately, that was the last of her progress. The pendant was a red jade donut on a short fourteen-karat gold chain given to her by her grandmother—heavy on sentimental value but not much else. Forensics had finished processing everything from the scene and came up blank—not a single piece of physical evidence to suggest someone else was in that apartment with Sarah Pullman at the time of her death. There wasn't even evidence of someone covering their tracks—nothing was void of fingerprints, which would at least tell Cerova someone had wiped something down.

It had been four days since Pullman's death, three since they found her body, and they didn't have any suspects or clues. Her life was fairly self-contained and revolved around work and derby. Between Collins and Cerova, they had tugged on every known connection and nothing had shaken out. Even Collins's gut didn't have any more hunches, and Cerova had come to respect her partner's instincts.

As the hour turned over, the early arrivals were just starting to trickle in. Cerova grabbed her binoculars and found familiar faces among the sizable turn out: Pullman's parents, some of her coworkers, and most of the Motor City Rollers. There were plenty of new faces, some which were easy identified as part of her derby family based on the bumper stickers plastered on their cars—Derby is my Jam, Roll or Die, My other wheels are quad skates, and lots of variation on I heart (or kiss) roller derby. There was even a Hello Kitty decked in skates and pads. The overwhelming image was the woman wearing tube socks and roller skates sitting in a martini glasses—the Detroit Roller Derby logo.

Cerova was just about to put away her binoculars when she recognized a tall brunette entering the funeral home—Agent Martinez of the FBI. She was dressed more casually and her wavy hair was down, but her bearing was still one of authority. Cerova wondered about the nature of her presence and considered the ramifications of asking Agent Martinez herself on the way out.

*****

Eleanor Pullman nervously twisted her used tissue in her hands as she paced the cold, sober halls of Plymouth Funeral Home. She appreciated how many people came to see Sadie, but there was only so many times she could hear "I'm sorry for your loss." She knew what was expected of her—to weakly nod, give a weak smile, and tell them "thank you."

It wasn't their fault; that's what one was supposed to do in this situation. They honesty believed they were comforting her when in reality, they were seeking their own catharsis. They needed Sadie to know they made an effort, and since she was dead, her family—by the transitive property—would suffice.

At least the mortician had done a good job on laying Sadie out. Her expression was peaceful, her makeup tasteful, and her posture natural. Eleanor picked out something that complimented her figure and coloring. She was glad that the last sight of her daughter wasn't on the slab at the morgue.

The further she moved away from Sadie's viewing, the quieter it got. Eleanor ducked into another cove and opened the first door she saw. There was a closed casket inside but no signs in the hall to indicate the room was in use. "I'm sorry," she apologized to the casket's occupant, even though she was fairly certain they took no offense. She took a seat in the back, and just when she thought she had no more tears left to cry, she found more. If she could, she would scream at the top of her lungs until the hurt left her, but she wasn't sure there was enough air for that. A mother should never have to bury her child.

Just breathe, she told herself.

Eleanor pulled out a new tissue and daubed her eyes when she heard the door open. "I'll be back in a second, James. I just needed a minute," she said without looking up.

"It's not James," Martinez spoke softly.

Eleanor stood up abruptly. "Oh, I'm sorry! Is this room supposed to be for yours? My daughter is down the hall, and I just had to get away."

"No, Ms. Pullman," Martinez reassured her and motioned for her to relax. "I was actually looking for you. I wanted to ask you some questions about Sarah."

"Oh," her voice fell as she sat back down. She didn't recognize this woman, but she certainly had the build of a derby player. "Were you a friend of Sadie's?"

"No, I didn't know her, but her friend Caroline Holt came to me for help." Eleanor heard sincerity in her voice that calmed her a measure.

"I know Caroline," Eleanor replied. "What kind of help?"

"Before Sarah died, she asked Caroline to keep something of hers safe, in case something happen to her. Caroline didn't know what to do with it, because she didn't understand how *special* Sarah was. The way she was special," Martinez said vaguely; if Mrs. Pullman was a magician, she would intimate her meaning.

"What on earth are you talking about?" Eleanor tried to dismiss Martinez, but the tremor in her tone belied her comprehension.

Martinez played it straight. "I think you know what I'm talking about, Ms. Pullman. I saw the mark on Sarah's shoulder, and unless I'm mistaken, you have a similar one."

Eleanor's body froze in place and her voice became quite frosty and precise. "Who are you?"

"Someone here to help find Sarah's killer if magic is involved in her untimely death," Martinez answered honestly.

"She was stabbed to death—that doesn't sound like magic to me," she pronounced with a shake her head.

"Perhaps, but if it was motivated by what Sarah was working on, the police are never going to find her murderer. But I can." Martinez let her words sink in. "Do you know what Sarah was up to?"

Eleanor fussed with her tissue, buying time to decide what to do with this mysterious stranger. "I only know what my daughter told me, which wasn't much on the best of days."

Martinez could see her close ranks—people wanted to protect the legacy of their dead. She made her own bluff. "Ms. Pullman, I've been to the drill hall."

Eleanor saw that jig was up and her facade collapsed. "I told her not to do it. 'Stay off the radar,' I told her. 'It's okay to use small magic and fix minor problems but the big stuff is dangerous,'" she parroted herself.

"Why did she do it?" Martinez continued the charade that she understood what Sarah had created.

"She was upset at the Masonic Temple for dropping the derby once the renovations were complete. They felt deeply betrayed, but there wasn't anything they could do about it."

"Except Sarah could," Martinez interjected.

"Exactly."

"But I thought it wasn't common knowledge that the Masons weren't going to renew the lease," Martinez countered.

"Sarah is…was on the derby council. They have known for months, but were holding off on making any announcements until they found a new place. Sarah was livid and wanted to hit them where it hurt," Eleanor explained.

"The Masons," Martinez stated emphatically.

Eleanor nodded. "She figured stripping the magic from the

enchanted items in the ritual tower would be just desserts and using their own methods against them was the cherry on top."

"Wait, I thought the Masons were phonies," Martinez replied. "Are you saying they *do* know how to wield magic?"

The older women smirked. "No more than they can turn lead into gold, but they figured out a way to use geometry to affect magic. That's their big secret—they know math. If you were to ask a Mason, the use of the circle in rituals was one of their inventions. Well, if you were male and a member of the brotherhood."

"Where did they get these magical items and how do you know about them?" Martinez queried.

"I assumed they gathered them over the years and hoarded them. There are always a few practitioners that mix with the Masons, despite the taboo, to help them identify things and figure out how to work them. Did you know they call them artifacts?" she said the word condescendingly. "As for how I know about them, my husband, Sarah's father, is a Mason. I stumbled upon a section of the tower during a painfully boring Masons' dinner—sometimes they hold 'bring your wife' nights."

Interesting—Sarah herself is a magic-Mason fusion, Martinez noted for later thought. "Is your husband a practitioner?" Martinez curiously asked.

"James?! Heaven's no! I don't think he even really believes magic is real. Like most Masons, he went for the fraternity and pageantry. It's the institutional version of guys in their forties telling each other about their glory days playing football in high school."

"And he didn't know about your and Sarah's abilities?" Martinez voiced her skepticism.

Eleanor's posture straightened. "My mother cautioned me to keep it a secret, much like I cautioned Sadie, only I listened to mother," she stressed. "There is a reason it is passed along the maternal line."

Martinez rolled with the resistance and changed topics. "I thought you said Sarah didn't tell you much, but this seems like a big secret."

Eleanor gave an honest but weary smile. "She had no choice. She needed my help."

Martinez leaned in. "How so?"

The older woman tilted her head. "I gave Sadie her father's copy of *Sacred Geometry* so she could figure out how to build it."

"Mrs. Pullman, you obviously had your reservations about this scheme," Martinez set up her last question. "Why did you help her?"

Eleanor shrugged and gestured with her hands, trying to conjure reason where none existed. "She was my child, the only one with my gift...my other kids are boys. She was so headstrong, and it was a strained relationship at the best of times, especially during her ill-conceived marriage. She rarely asked me for anything, much less for my help. I know it sounds crazy, but this summer was the closest we had been in a long time."

*****

Meridiana slipped in with the herd of other skaters as they exchanged platitudes. *I can't believe it. She was so young. She will be missed. It's such a tragedy. Her poor parents.* The only sentiment Meridiana did not find insipid was *I hope they gut the SOB that did this to her.*

Most people drifted in, exchanged muted pleasantries and stepped up to the casket. Those that knew Sadie very well paid their respects to her family. She guessed on average fifteen minutes door-to-door. Meridiana, on the other hand, bided her time. Eventually, the crowd thinned and there was no one waiting to see Sadie.

She was both nervous and excited. If it worked, it would be the first time in over a thousand years. All she needed was a touch, and she found the buildup exhilarating. Her heart beat quickened as she approached the casket until she finally reached Sadie—her hands were folded over her chest, and she really did look like she was sleeping.

The succubus extended her will and touched Sadie's cold hand. Suddenly, Meridiana was somewhere else, somewhere behind another person's eyes. She was standing at a table, running a circular blade over fabric. She didn't have to think about it, she was just doing it. A cold wind blew past her, and she shivered. As she breathed in, she smelled something faint but familiar.

Her point of view shifted, reminding the succubus that she was merely an observer in this play, not the actor. She saw a shadow along her outstretched arm, and when she looked up, she saw a headless mannequin welding a pair of stork scissors. Fear coursed through her and all she could think was, "Oh God, I don't want to die."

Meridiana broke contact abruptly, and much to her bewilderment, she was crying. She flinched at the gentle hand placed on her shoulder. She heard a concerned voice on the other end, "Are you okay?" Meridiana turned and found herself face-to-face with Martinez.

"Yeah, just a little overwhelmed, but it's passing." She wiped away the tears and lightened her tone, "Fancy running into you here."

"I could say the same about you," Martinez played nice. "Why don't we take a seat in the back and catch up." Once they found a private nook, she started with the obvious question, "How do you know Sarah Pullman?"

"We're on the same derby team," Meridiana answered.

Martinez raised a quizzical brow. "Pro-dom and derby?"

"I can take as good as I can give," she retorted. "#142, Scarlet Leather."

It took a second for Martinez to dredge up the reference. "Wasn't Hester Prynne a Puritan? An odd provenance for a derby name."

"Not so odd. She was a woman condemned by her community for falling in love with a man of the cloth," Meridiana defended.

"Okay, that tracks," Martinez conceded, "although I seriously doubt she did it in leather."

"No one's perfect," the succubus quipped.

"So Sarah wasn't a friend-friend like Janice Keller?" Martinez asked.

"No. She wasn't my type. A little too pixie for me," Meridiana stated plainly. "And what brings *you* here?"

"I'm here to figure out who put Sarah in that very expensive wooden box," Martinez spoke in a low voice.

Meridiana's whole demeanor changed. "What are you doing tonight?"

"Why?" Martinez suspiciously asked.

"Can you come by the club tonight? I may have pertinent information that will be utterly useless to the Detroit PD," she spoke in a hushed tone.

"Can't you just tell me here?" Martinez whispered, keeping watch for anyone getting too close.

"I'd rather speak somewhere *safer*," Meridiana emphasized.

Martinez petulantly responded, "You know, if you were a character in a Hercule Poirot story, the next scene would be you getting killed before you could tell me what you know."

Meridiana smirked. "I didn't know you cared, Teresa."

Martinez sighed. "What time?"

"10:00 p.m. My first appointment doesn't start until eleven."

"Don't die before ten," Martinez whispered firmly.

"I'll try my best."

Chapter Fourteen

Detroit, Michigan, USA
26th of September, 7:50 p.m. (GMT-4)

It was dark, cold and raining when Martinez left the funeral home. She hadn't brought an umbrella and made a mad dash for her Hellcat. She started the engine and turned on the heater and defroster before checking her phone. There was no word from Chloe and Dot, but the analysts had come through on Samuel Johnson—his closest living relative was his younger sister, Abigail Johnson Morales, who lived out of state. If she didn't already know karma was a thing, she would have thought it was simply serendipity. *Then again, I wouldn't be in this situation if I weren't Salt Mine*, she reframed her victory.

She put in a request for supporting documentation and if all went according to plan, she should have her time with Johnson tomorrow. Next, she sent a message to the librarians through a secure protocol in hopes that knowing Sarah Pullman's intent could help them decipher her journal. She wondered if the Salt Mine even knew the Masons had magic items.

She was driving out of the parking lot when she noticed a dark blue compact car parked in the far back of the lot. It was one among a cluster, probably where the employees parked to leave the spaces upfront for visitors and patrons. However, this vehicle had a driver sitting in the dark. The way her headlights caught glass and reflected, Martinez guessed they were using a pair of binoculars.

Martinez circled back around and pulled up to the driver's side window. She motioned for the woman in the other vehicle to roll her window down. Cerova complied. "Nice night for a stake out. Or do you make a habit of stalking funeral homes?"

"Thursday night at the Plymouth is a happening place," Cerova casually replied.

"Did you see anything interesting?"

"Just a bunch of friends and family…" Cerova trailed off.

"And an FBI agent," Martinez finished her sentence.

"Indulge a fellow law enforcement officer—are you here in a personal or professional capacity?" Cerova tested the waters.

"If I were here on FBI business, I would have my badge out," Martinez responded. "Why? Are you having concerns with a case that warrant FBI intervention?"

"No. I'm good," Cerova quickly answered. "But if you find out anything that would help me catch Sarah Pullman's killer, I'd appreciate a heads up."

"Naturally. Anything for a fellow law enforcement officer," Martinez graciously replied. "Have a good night, Detective Cerova." She rolled up her window and eased off the brakes.

Martinez kept her eyes on her rear-view mirror and drove a circuitous route home to ensure she wasn't being followed.

The last thing she needed was Cerova to know where she lived and make any connection between Tessa Marvel and Teresa Martinez.

The rain had let up by the time she got home, and her stomach growled at the smell of chicken noodle soup and fresh baked bread that saturated the air. "I'm home. Smells good."

"Pot's still on the stove, and I made Parker House rolls," Stigma answered from the couch. When he looked up and saw Martinez, his tone changed to admonishment. "You're soaked. Go get into some dry clothes before you catch pneumonia."

"Yes, Mom," she dourly responded in her best impersonation of Dot. Once in her room, she stripped off her wet clothes and hung them up in her bathroom. She toweled off as much water as she could and freshened up her makeup—heavy on the eyeliner and dark lipstick. She took the pins out of the hair and tousled it back to life. Then she changed her bra to something less supportive and more lifting. Once she was sure her legs were completely dry, she slid into a pair of leather pants and a low cut top. When she descended the stairs, Stigma did a double take. "I'm flattered by the effort, but I was fine with flannel pajamas."

She gave him a patronizing look. "I'm going back out, but not before I get some food." She disappeared into the kitchen and came back with a bowl of soup, a salad, and two buttered rolls. "What did I miss?"

"Well, little miss 'I thought we had something!' didn't get a rose. Surprise, surprise," Stigma answered and stared in awe at how Martinez managed to eat without spilling on her leather or her cleavage. "It's a booty call, isn't it?"

"Who makes a booty call at 9:00 p.m. on a weeknight?" she asked incredulously.

"Sad people who have work in the morning but still need love?" he took a stab in the dark.

She laughed. "I was asked to stop by 18 is 9."

"All this is for Aloysius?" he asked in disbelief.

"Fitting in is part of the cover," she replied between bites. "I can't very well go in looking like an FBI agent or a soccer mom."

"You're right, but at least use a bib. Watching you eat is making me nervous, and it would be a shame to get soup spatter on any of that."

*****

Meridiana sat at her vanity, having a stiff drink and trying to make sense of the night. As a general rule, it took a lot to make her cry real tears, not the crocodile ones she turn on and off as succubus. She could easily count the number of times she'd genuinely cried on one hand. Hell was not a friendly place, and devils had a very different notion of what it took to raise a successful brood. The depths of fiendish punishment, treachery, vengeance, pettiness, and hatred were unfathomable to most humans.

It wasn't that devils didn't have feelings; they just perceived them differently than mortals. Provided they weren't culled at a young age or assassinated for their ambition, fiends were long-lived and processed things in an extended frame of view. Devils couldn't be too bothered by the small stuff, and a large swath of what mortals considered important was of minor note on the grand scale of things.

By comparison, humans were just manic gnats when it came to feelings. After a millennia of being exiled among them, Meridiana speculated their limited life spans were to blame. It compressed everything into a shorter time, effectively concentrating all their emotions. Everything they felt, they felt immensely before flitting to the next emotion, which utterly consumed them until the next one, and the next one—ad infinitum until their brief lives came to an end. When she was still in Hell's fold, she found it an exhausting nuisance.

But that was before she had gotten her first taste of love. She was intoxicated by it. It was like gorging on a thousand souls, only better. She had never reached such heady heights before, nor ever quite since then. She had long considered her curse the price for such joy, but now she knew better. Tonight, she had finally caught a glimpse of what the specter of death felt like though a human's eyes, and it was terrifying.

Meridiana should have been pleased. She had reclaimed a piece of her old power, but it came with a catch—she could no longer avoid empathy in the maneuver. In the past, she could know what her targets knew without also feeling their emotions. *Touché, curse*, she toasted her beautiful reflection.

Emotions aside, there were other objective differences. Typically, Meridiana could access all sorts of memories and thoughts, even if she could only watch one scene at a time. With Sadie, there was no navigating her mind. Perhaps it was because she was dead, but she could never rule out a fundamental change post-curse. Either way, she wasn't in a rush to test the boundaries and relive that again.

Now that she was no longer connected to Sadie, Meridiana could replay the clip in her mind and analyze each detail without the distraction of emotions. She took a calculated risk by inviting a Salt Mine agent into her affairs, but as the saying goes—the enemy of my enemy is my friend.

She was lost in thought and memories when a knock fell on her door. She consulted the clock on the wall. *Where had the time gone?* the succubus asked herself rhetorically. She was still in her dressing gown; she'd have to get ready while they talked. "Come in," Meridiana called out as she brushed her hair.

Martinez opened the door but didn't immediately cross the threshold, sending her will out to check for traps. Amused, Meridiana started pinning up her long tresses and allowed the agent to wander inside in her own time. Eventually, Martinez stepped into the dressing room and closed the door. She grabbed the chair along the side of the wall and took a seat to the side of the pro-dom. "So, what did you want to talk about?" she started the conversation.

Meridian took the last bobby pin from her mouth and jammed it along her scalp. "I know what killed Sarah Pullman."

Martinez honed in on the word "what." "Pray tell," she invited more information.

"It was her mannequin," Meridiana said decisively as she checked the back of her hair with a handheld mirror and her vanity. "Stabbed her with her own scissors."

"You're telling me an inanimate object plunged a pair of scissors into Sarah Pullman's chest?" Martinez repeated for clarity.

"I'm just telling you Sadie saw," Meridiana answered before creating a quick smokey eye.

With some dread, Martinez spoke, "But that would mean I'm looking for—"

"Yup," the succubus commiserated. "Have fun hunting down an animator."

"Damn it," Martinez cursed. She had an academic knowledge of magicians that specialized in bringing inanimate objects to life, but had never gone up against one. They usually stuck to small things—think the sorcerer's apprentice before he became mad with power. They put a little piece of their will into a simple object for a discrete task.

The more accomplished animators could do more complex things with intricate objects, like permanently bind a piece of themselves into an object and create a facsimile of life, such as constructs and golems. The more complex animations could sort of work things out within set parameters, but they are generally designed to take orders.

The most expert of animators could take a piece of their soul and create life itself within an object—think Pinocchio. Of course, splitting your soul into pieces generally drives people insane, so maybe more like He Who Must Not Be Named, except he was pure fiction and master animators were real.

Whoever was controlling that mannequin was asking it to do more than mop some floors, but it wasn't actively magical when she was inside Pullman's apartment after the fact—that put her animator somewhere between better than novice but not a master. She did take solace in the fact that as least she had a good idea of who the magician was and that he was living in a locked ward. This was one animator she didn't have to track down.

"Okay, nothing I can't handle," Martinez spoke after she got a grip on the situation.

Meridiana pulled out her liquid eyeliner. "Oh, there's more."

Martinez steadied herself. "I'm listening."

"There's a fiend involved," she said between tracing her lids in black.

"How do you know that?" Martinez quizzed her.

"When I was in the moment with Sadie, I smelled what she

smelled, only my sense of smell is more discerning than hers. Right before she was attacked, I smelled a whiff of aether." She blinked her eyes a few times before moving on to her blush.

"Could you tell who it was?" Martinez inquired.

The succubus threw her a brusque look via the mirror. "What do you think we are—dogs? We don't mark with scent so we can walk by and say 'oh, Belial was here.'"

"I'm just asking," Martinez held up her hands. "I don't know how these things work—no offense intended."

Meridiana muttered "Ignorant" under her breath and applied a dark red matte to her lips.

"So this is something you can do…see through people's eyes?" Martinez broached the subject carefully.

"Apparently, in this case, it wasn't evil, but generally no, I can't," she rubbed her lips together. "Navigating morality is a nightmare—such a slim line between not evil and totally evil."

"How exactly does all that work? With your curse, I mean," Martinez clarified.

Meridiana shrugged her shoulders. "If I can do it, it's not evil. If it is, I can't." She cinched up her stockings and unrolled them up her shapely legs. "It's very similar to what humans do. Might makes right, ordeals by contest, history is written by the victors and all that jazz."

"Except humans are capable of doing evil," Martinez pointed out.

"I didn't make the rules," Meridiana lamented as she

rose and went behind her privacy screen. Her body from the shoulders down disappeared.

Martinez wondered aloud. "Why are you telling *me?*"

"I don't like the female magician body count in my near proximity," she answered simply as she disrobed and tossed the silk garment over the screen.

"Any fiends got an axe to grind with you?" Martinez switched gears.

A fleeting thought crossed her mind but she pushed it back for now. "I've been out of the game for a millennia. I'm the turtle at the bottom of the stack. I'm not worth the time." She slipped her underskirt on before putting on her boots.

Martinez decided to take her at her word and reanalyzed the situation—there wasn't a trace of demon or devil activity on Pullman, in her apartment, or at the drill hall. Whatever fiend was involved had to be through the animator. Things weren't looking good for Samuel Johnson. "I caught a detective parked outside the funeral home tonight. What sort of questions have they asked you?"

Meridiana zipped up her boots, whipped her corset around her torso, and hooked the front. "The run-of-the-mill questions: how well did we know her, do we know of anyone that would want to hurt her, was she acting strange in the past couple of days or weeks, was she seeing anyone, any problems at work or derby, yada, yada, yada…" Meridiana expertly eased the laces behind her back, pulling them in the middle and distributing the tension with her fingers as she spoke.

"Anything stick out as unusual? Specific?" Martinez reframed the question.

Meridiana tied the ends in a bow and tucked them under the modesty panel for a clean finish. "They did ask about her necklace."

"Her necklace?" Martinez confirmed.

"Yeah, Sadie always wore a red jade donut on the short chain. They brought pictures of it to practice yesterday and asked if she was wearing it at practice on Sunday." Meridiana reemerged from behind the screen as Mistress Scarlet.

"And was she?" Martinez followed up.

Meridiana selected a riding crop from the wall. "Yeah, she always wore it."

Martinez objected, "She wasn't wearing it tonight."

Meridiana thought back and frowned. "No, she wasn't."

Chapter Fifteen

Detroit, Michigan, USA
27th of September, 12:15 a.m. (GMT-4)

By all accounts, Harold Weber should have been in bed two hours ago. He wasn't a young man anymore, but he could never pass up a good puzzle. Even though his hair was gray and his glasses thick, his mind was as sharp as a tack, and his blue eyes never sparkled brighter than when he was in the midst of a conundrum.

He knew any attempt at sleep would be fretful, with dreams full of ellipses and equations. All other things being equal, he would rather press on. Plus, he had just made a new pot of tea, and Chloe and Dot had brought pumpkin spice creamer. He couldn't say he was as fond of it as the twins, but it went nice with a strong builder's tea and shortbread, which the Salt Mine always had in supply for entering the Magh Meall.

The three of them stared at Weber's chalkboards, all five of them. Chloe and Dot had painstakingly transcribed everything from the journal so they could visualize the whole of Sarah Pullman's work at once. The geometry was simple enough: three tangential circles inside of an ellipse to which they also touched. Anyone with a compass could have done that. Imbuing the lines with magic, again, was nothing spectacular. Still, they were uncertain how it was supposed to operate and to what end. Even the message from Lancer was less than helpful: *Sarah Pullman, father mason, mother magician, wanted to strip magic from mason's magical artifacts in ritual tower; motive: revenge.*

According to Chloe and Dot, there were prescribed ways of nullifying magical items. You could shield them in warded circles and/or insulate them in non-inert material. This was the preferred method of the Salt Mine, whose lower levels housed many neutralized items, and why agents packed things in salt for transport. If they were rune-based, like saltcasters, you simply disrupted the rune or destroyed the base material. For items with a finite power supply, you could exhaust its power, like draining a battery. If it was powered by a spirit, you could free the spirit—the equivalent of taking the batteries out. You could hurl it into a different plane, like they had tried to do with the original mirror that drew the attention of the outsider known to the Sumerians as the Hallow. And the most extreme measure was to obliterate it, but the kind of energy required for that would probably kill its wielder unless it was a legendary creature, like a god or one of the elder fae.

Weber dunked another wedge of shortbread into his tea. "We're missing something."

"You've said that already, Harold," muttered Dot, who was taking a break from banging her head on the table to merely resting on it.

"I'll stop saying it once it's no longer true," he said stubbornly. "There's a lot of math there for simple geometry. That's the ticket. I'm sure of it."

"Harold, we've cross-referenced with all your science books. They don't look like any of the equations Pullman was working with," Chloe insisted.

Weber refused to accept defeat. "Hand me her journal. We're missing something."

Dot gave her sister a look that roughly translated as *I will kill him if he says that one more time.* Chloe answered with a smile that said *Patience.* Chloe passed the journal to the German.

Weber had been an engineer in his previous life, before Leader found him and gave him free rein to tinker. Even as a child, he was constantly taking things apart to see how they worked, much to his parents' consternation. Most of the time, he'd put them back together. Sometimes he'd improved upon them. When he'd developed the ability to practice the arts in his adolescence, it simply became another widget or tool for him to build with.

It was his familiarity with the realms of engineering, science, and mathematics that prompted Chloe and Dot to ask for his help. They knew just about everything there was to know about the arcane, and while they could recall the equations with their eidetic memories, they had no meaning without knowing how to apply them and to what effect. For that, they needed an engineer.

Weber was making old man noises as he flipped through pages of costumes and patterns when he abruptly stopped. "What's this?" He pointed to the page. "This oval isn't on the chalkboard."

Chloe looked over his shoulder. "It's a derby play. Xs are blockers and O is the jammer."

Weber only understood half the words that came out of her mouth and started at the beginning. "What's derby?"

Chloe cut down on the lingo and went with simpler terms. "It's a game of chase on roller skates. There are two teams, and only one person on each team is allowed to score points. Each team wants to help their scorer skate around the track the most times while also blocking the other team's scorer by getting in their way or knocking them out of bounds with their body."

"So there are skaters going around and around on this oval?" Weber asked.

"Yes," Chloe answered.

"How many skaters?"

"Each team is allowed five skaters on the track at a time, but there are fourteen on a team, because people get hurt or get pulled from the track for penalties," Chloe replied.

Weber started flipping through the journal and looking back and forth to the chalkboards. "How high do the scores get in these games?"

Dot raised her head and suddenly became very interested in this line of query. Unless she was mistaken, Weber was onto something. "Usually in the hundreds on each side if they are doing a full bout."

"And that correlates to completed laps?" Weber picked up a piece of chalk and started writing things down on the least-congested board.

"No. Points are scored based on how many of the other team's players the scorer passes after the first lap, but each team has four members who are skating around the track the whole time. Their laps don't go toward the score," Chloe puzzled at the question.

A lightness of being came over the inventor and he laughed out loud. "That brilliant young woman! I wish I could have talked to her before her untimely death."

"You want to fill the rest of the class in, Harold?" Dot chimed in.

"We've been looking at this all wrong. It's not magic. It's technology. If you look at it like electricity, the math adds up. *That's* what I was missing—the skaters!"

The twins looked at each other and neither knew how to parse that. "Harold, we need you to use more words. Walk us through it," Chloe gently brought him back to their level.

"Faraday figured out that if you pass a magnet through an electromagnetic field, you can create electricity. This young lady did the same thing, except instead of a magnet, she used the will of the skaters and instead of an electromagnetic field, she created a magical field."

Dot searched for the closest corollary. "Like ley lines?"

"Yes, but those are naturally occurring. She created it using her own magic and locked it in place using masonic principles," he spoke in as simple of terms as he could muster. "Every time one of those skaters completes a circuit around the oval, they generate magical energy."

"Like an induction coil?" Chloe stepped out on a limb.

"Exactly!" Weber exclaimed. He walked over to a column of numbers. "See? She calculated how much energy each skater would make with a complete circuit and multiplied that by each participant in the game." His blue eyes widened. "What direction do they skate?"

"Generally counter-clockwise," Chloe answered.

Weber clapped his hands and giggled. "She even put in an amplifier, so no matter where a skater starts their circuit, it will feed back into the circles, growing geometrically as it passes through each loop."

"But what about karmic cost?" Dot asked.

"There's no magic being conducted, only magical energy being created. They don't even have to be magicians to power this thing. It's just the movement and will of the skaters," Weber explained. "I'm assuming as a sport, it gets highly competitive?"

Dot smirked, thinking about the takedowns she had witnessed. "That's a hard yes," she affirmed.

"So, Sarah figured out a way to capture the energy that was already being expended in playing the sport and turn it into magical energy at no karmic cost?" Chloe slowly followed his train of thought.

"Precisely," Weber complimented her comprehension.

"But isn't that dangerous? Like when live power lines get knocked down?" Dot said thoughtfully.

"Ah, that's where this comes in." Weber walked to the second chalkboard and circled a set of equations. "She channeled the energy to some sort of a magical resistor. I'll have to work out the math, but she did anticipate a loss of energy in the transfer."

"I hate to be a wet blanket, but how is this supposed to strip the magic from the Mason's artifacts?" Dot came to the crux of the problem.

"Don't you see? She wasn't going to remove or nullify magic. She was going to short-circuit them with more magic," Weber exalted the ingenuity. "As soon as she turned off the resistor, all the pent-up energy would release at once, like a magical electromagnetic pulse. The subsequent wave would fry anything magical in a wave emanating from the oval."

"She built a bomb!" Dot finally glommed onto his train of thought.

"Yes, a *magical* bomb!" Weber declared triumphantly in the thrill of solving a stubborn puzzle.

"Starting with the Ritual Temple right next door to the drill hall," Chloe muttered with less enthusiasm as the others. She turned to Weber. "Do you have map of Detroit?"

Weber rummaged through one of his numerous drawers

until he found the right one. Chloe unfolded the oversized paper and found Temple Street. "Hand me a ruler," she requested to no one in particular and held out her hand until someone complied. She drew a straight edge from the Masonic Temple to Zug Island and did some quick mental math. "Zug Island is less than five miles from the Masonic Temple as the crow flies."

She turned to Dot, who was responsible for buying their season tickets. "When does derby season start?"

"First game is right before Halloween, but they usually start practicing in the drill hall in October," she answered.

Chloe started handing out assignments. "Harold, can you work out this math and see what kind of energy we are dealing with in real, applicable terms? Dot, contact Martinez and let her know what we've pieced together. Then start a worst-case scenario based on Harold's numbers in terms of impact on the magical community."

"What are you going to do?" Dot asked.

"I'm going to comb through every inch of this journal for a hint of what this resistor could be."

Dot corrected her sister, "More like a detonator."

Chapter Sixteen

Ann Arbor, Michigan, USA
27th of September, 9:35 a.m. (GMT-4)

The morning bustle clipped by at a familiar pace at Evergreen Meadows, a premier senior community offering a seamless transition to skilled nursing should the need ever arise. Many began their residence in one of the independent living apartments, decorated with treasured items that made the cut when the elderly finally decided to downsize. There was maintenance on-site as well as skilled nursing staff should home visits become necessary. For those that required around-the-clock care or supervision, there was a live-in facility.

The concept was sold to families as the perfect solution for the seniors in their lives: they could live as independently as possible in their golden years while having a safety net. However, the residents of Evergreen Meadows knew what moving in meant—this was their last stop. Still, they didn't complain; this was one of the nicer places, and their families hadn't put them somewhere cheaper in a bid to preserve their inheritance.

While the active seniors lived on their own schedules, the other residents in the facility had more regimented days. Meals marked the passage of time in this part of Evergreen Meadows, especially for the staff. It was nothing short of directing a staged production three times a day: assisting in ablutions, administering insulin to the diabetics, corralling everyone to the dining room, getting food served, helping those eat that needed it, and getting everyone back into places with cleaning and toileting as necessary. Of course, residents had the option of eating in their rooms, but the staff always encouraged socialization in the dining room.

Emily Peel, LPN, was taking a short break in that magic time between meals; everyone was where they were supposed to be and it wasn't yet time to start the process for the next one. She had spent most of her nursing career working with the geriatric population and loved her job, but even the best of days could run one ragged. She lived by the principle that everyone could use a smile and a kind word, especially in the worst of times, but all that positivity had a carrying cost. In her thirty years, she'd learned to allow herself these moments to get off her feet, drink something, have a snack of her own, and regroup.

She flipped through Pinterest until she finished her coffee and yogurt, washed her hands, and left the quiet of the break room. "I'm back," Peel announced to the woman sitting at the nurse's station.

"Thank God! I have to pee so bad," her coworker declared in a low whisper.

"We could always cath you or give you an adult brief," Peel joked in the humor one could only use with other nurses.

She received a cold stare for her effort. "I'm old, but I'm not that old."

Peel covered the desk while her colleague took a break, and started pulling patient records. Dr. Walker wouldn't be here for another fifteen minutes, which gave her plenty of time to prepare things as he liked them. First, she grabbed the files on all the residents who needed their routine checkups as required by Medicare. Then, she compiled the list of patients with new complaints or worrisome changes. The doctor only came once a week, and she had to make the most of the time they had him.

The bell chimed as Martinez entered the front door dressed in a modest tunic and slacks with her oversized leather bag. The lobby was clean and decorated with fresh-cut flowers and potted plants to give the appearance of life, despite the overwhelming smell of potpourri to cover the odor of industrial medicinal cleaner. Martinez knew the smell well: the alcohol of the hand sanitizer liberally available in all health care settings.

Peel looked up. "Can I help you?"

Martinez smiled. "Yes, I'm here to visit a resident, Samuel Johnson."

Peel nodded with a smile. "May I ask how you know Mr. Johnson?"

"I'm his niece. I just moved to the area earlier this year, and my mom has asked me to look in on him. I took the morning off, because she said he might get more agitated as the day wears on," she explained.

"I see. Can you tell me your mother's name?" Peel asked firmly but politely.

"Of course." Martinez brushed back her bangs. "Abigail Morales."

Peel typed away and kept her eyes on her computer screen. "And your name?"

"Tiffany Morales," she answered.

"Would you like me to add your name to the visitor's list? It will save some time in future visits," Peel added.

"Sure," Martinez agreed.

"Do you have some sort of photo ID?"

"I haven't gotten my Michigan driver's license yet. Is my work badge okay?" she asked politely.

Peel smiled reassuringly. "Anything with your name and picture will work." Martinez handed the fake ID the Salt Mine had cooked up overnight, and Peel entered it into the computer.

Peel rose from her chair. She was short and plump with the same short no-nonsense haircut all nurses of a certain age get at one time or another. "Follow me." She strode down the hall with purpose in her scrubs and white leather shoes, surprisingly fast for someone that couldn't have been more than five feet tall.

She talked as they walked, the habit of people that are often asked to do more with less time. "Your uncle is in the dementia wing. We have locked doors that require a code to open so residents don't wander off. I'll let you in and take you to his room. When you're ready to leave, one of the nurses in that wing will open the door for you. Make sure the door closes behind you."

Martinez looked away but kept the number pad in her periphery. The code was four digits: the month and the year—something simple the staff could remember but something a person with dementia wouldn't put together. "How has my uncle been?" she made conversation.

Peel bobbed her head side-to-side. "He's generally in good spirits, but he had an incident last weekend that required intervention. He's calmed down since then and we've been keeping a close eye on him."

"What kind of incident?" Martinez asked.

"Sunday night, he woke up screaming and thrashing. We tried to calm him down but eventually we had to call the doctor," Peel answered—it was always on the weekends or in the middle of the night, and Lord help you if it coincided with a full moon. "After we got him to sleep, he was fine. Didn't even remember it the next morning."

Peel paused in the hall a few doorways from his room. "Has it been a while since you've seen him?"

"Years," Martinez answered. "But I brought some family photos and clips from his old TV show. I thought maybe we could sit together and go through them, if he's feeling up to it."

Peel approved; the girl, or perhaps her mother, had done her homework.   "Okay, so we'll introduce you as a visitor and see if he remembers you. Don't be offended if he doesn't. It's not him; it's the Alzheimer's. If he gets agitated, don't try to challenge him or correct him. Just let him be and hit the button for the nurse," Peel prepped Martinez before continuing the last five feet to Mr. Johnson's room.

Just before she knocked, she put on a smile and her round face lit up. "Good morning, Mr. Johnson! You have a visitor."

Martinez summoned her will and followed behind her. The first thing she checked the room for was wards, but there were none.

The room was surprisingly cozy and cheerful. The adjustable hospital bed was made and a colorful quilt covered it. There was a small desk with framed photos and a few knick-knacks. Beside the desk was a bookcase with rows of spines. Apparently, Johnson was quite the reader at one time. The TV mounted to the wall was on, playing a rerun of a crime procedural that hadn't been on prime time for at least twenty years. In the recliner opposite the screen was Samuel Johnson.

"Hello there, young lady!" he greeted Peel. "It must be my lucky day—I get a girl for each arm." He chortled at his own joke. He was older with more wrinkles and loose skin, but Martinez recognized the smile and twinkle in his eyes as the same as in the picture in his file from all those decades ago. He turned his attention to her. "And who are you?"

Martinez dropped to one knee so they were eye-to-eye. "It's me, Uncle Sam, Tiffany. Abby's girl?" She cast her will at him, probing him as he processed. He seemed nice enough, but if he were under a fiendish influence, he could be dangerous without even knowing it.

A moment of confusion flickered across his face but he quickly plastered a smile over it. "I have a sister named Abby," he stated.

"That's right," Peel affirmed. "This is her daughter, Tiffany."

"I'd like to sit with you, and I've brought some things we could look at together. Or we can just watch TV together?" Martinez played along and kept her spell up.

Johnson shrugged his shoulders. "I've never said no to the company of a pretty girl." Martinez wasn't sure what to make of this. Either Johnson was going along with the lie, he honestly didn't know his sister didn't have a daughter, or he couldn't remember and was playing along. People with dementia were notoriously good at covering up their deficits.

With permission granted, Martinez mouthed a silent "thank you" to Peel. The nurse acknowledged it and addressed Mr. Johnson again. "I have to go and meet the doctor now, Mr. Johnson. You two have a good visit, and the doctor may want to see you today."

Johnson dismissively waved his hand. "You keep your doctor. I'm fine."

Martinez approached his desk to pull out the chair and did a sweep of what was out in plain sight. "I haven't seen some of these pictures before," she gave herself an excuse to snoop further. "You were so young and handsome."

"Young lady, I know that is supposed to be a compliment, but the last thing an old man wants to hear is what he used to be," he playfully chastised her.

Another flag went off in Martinez's mind—did he call all women young lady because he couldn't remember their names or if he hadn't met them before? Her grandfather had done something similar. All men were "feller" and ladies were "girly."

Martinez continued to engage him while probing with her will. "Now you're just fishing for compliments," she teased back. She looked at the titles on the bookshelves. "Do you still like to read?"

He harrumphed. "They don't write them like they used to. Every book I pick up, I can't seem to finish."

Closer to the bookshelf, one title stood out: *Sacred Geometry*. The same book the Chloe and Dot had turned to for answers and Sarah Pullman used to make whatever was in the drill hall. "What's this one about?" She pulled it out and presented it to Johnson as if they were going to read it together.

"Hey now, that's not for the purview of women. Those are Mason secrets," he corrected her. *That, he remembers*, Martinez noted as she put the book back on the shelf.

"How about we look through some pictures," she suggested.

She positioned her seat next to his recliner and pulled out her phone. She opened the gallery that the analysts created for her, which included all the pictures from his file, photos from his TV show, completely random pictures that were age appropriate, as well as pictures of Sarah Pullman. It was a test of sorts, and like a spider's web, Martinez had laid out her will to pick up the smallest esoteric tremor.

Johnson did well with the older pictures, filling in names, places, and context from the real photos and quickly dismissing the fakes with a wave of his hand. He still pretended to remember them, just that he wasn't interested in going over them today. Martinez weaved and bobbed to probe him during the process, but it was convoluted—what should have been straight lines and junctions were knots and dead ends.

As Martinez flipped to the picture of Sarah Pullman, Johnson lost his smile and went pale. Martinez felt a tug on one of her feelers. "Do you remember her?"

"It can't be. It was just a dream. She isn't real," he said rapidly.

"Where do you remember her from?" Martinez nudged him with her words but not her will, which was in knots at this point. If Johnson were more stable, she would have pressed but by this point, there was little doubt in her mind that Samuel Johnson was not all cognitively there.

"Knock, knock," a deep voice came from the hallway. The slim spectacled man in his fifties dressed in khakis and a polo shirt entered the room. He had a file in one hand, a stethoscope in the other, and Nurse Peel in tow. "I heard you had company, Mr. Johnson. You lucky devil."

"That's my young lady you're talking about. Don't go trying anything funny," Johnson joked. Whatever recognition she had stumbled upon was gone but Martinez kept her will extended and still like an ambush predator.

He raised his hands in surrender. "I wouldn't dream of it, Mr. Johnson. Is it okay for us to talk about how you're doing with your visitor here?"

Johnson nodded. "She's all right."

The doctor extended his hand. "I'm Dr. Walker."

"I'm his niece, Tiffany," she replied as she shook his hand.

Walker smiled warmly before flipping through the chart Peel had handed him moments earlier. "Everything looks good. Are you having any pain or problems urinating?"

"You should be so lucky to pee as well as I do at my age," Johnson remarked.

"Any fever, change in appetite, increased incontinence, or confusion?" he asked Peel.

"No report of any from the nurses," she answered.

Walker unwound the stethoscope, put the earpieces in, and rubbed the bell between his hands to warm it. "I'm just going to do a quick exam," he prefaced before snaking the bell up Johnson's shirt. "I'm listening to your heart, so you can just stay still…. Good, now take a deep breath in…and again."

The doctor moved to the back. "Another deep breath… and once more." Then he moved the bell to Johnson's lower stomach. "Don't mind me, just want to see how breakfast is doing," he joked. Peel smiled even though Martinez was pretty sure it was the umpteenth time the nurse had heard that one.

Walker took off the earpieces, wound up the stethoscope, and tucked it into his pocket. "I'm just going to press on your stomach. Tell me if anything hurts when I do." He quickly pressed in deep but released just as quickly in two or three places. "Anything?"

"You keep going and you're going to have to buy me dinner, young man," Johnson quipped.

"I'm glad you're feeling well enough to make jokes, Mr. Johnson," Walker replied as he scribbled some notes in the chart. "Do you have any questions for me, Mr. Johnson?"

"When am I getting out of here?" Johnson asked earnestly.

Walker smiled. "You're here for your safety, Mr. Johnson. How about you, niece Tiffany? Do you have any questions for me?"

"Just one," she piped up. "What happened this weekend?"

Walker's expression changed from folksy to clinical in the blink of an eye. "Sunday evening, your uncle had a psychotic episode where he believed he saw things that weren't there. The staff tried to calm him down, but ultimately, we had to give him a sedative for his own safety. It can happen in dementia patients, and my concern was that it stemmed from a urinary tract infection. I tested his urine and started him on a short round of antibiotics. Things seem to have cleared up."

"All this talk about my pee is making me need to go." Johnson leaned forward in his chair and grabbed his walker. All three of them immediately tried to help, and he shooed them away. "I'm losing my marbles, not my ability to take a piss."

Martinez saw her chance. "Thank you, Doctor. I'll wait for him to finish. You guys can continue your work."

Peel was already readying the next chart while Walker made his excuses, "Have a nice day, Mr. Johnson, niece Tiffany." The doctor closed the door behind him.

"Would you like me to give you a hand?" Martinez offered once they were out of the room. She interpreted Johnson's grumble as an affirmative. She positioned herself at Johnson's side, and braced the walker with one leg. He put his hands on the walker and on the count of three, he stood and she assisted in that effort. It was a maneuver she had done for her grandfather many times before in another life.

Once he was out of the recliner and had a hold of his walker, he was pretty steady on his feet. He slowly plodded to his bathroom and closed the door once inside. As soon as she heard him take a seat on the commode, Martinez pulled out her vape pen and cast salt throughout the room. She didn't have the luxury of time to do them serially. Luckily, it was a small room.

She waited for magical patterns to shake themselves out

while the sound of Johnson's urine stream started. The salt in Johnson's recliner revealed his signature. She snapped a picture and used the broad side of her hand to brush aside as much of the salt as possible.

The salt on Johnson's bed was a different matter. It was mostly Johnson's signature, but there were definite spots of interference. Martinez had seen it before on her first case in the Salt Mine in the former, demon-possessed coroner for Chiltern Hills in the United Kingdom. Unless it was early days in the possession, she seriously doubted it was a demon—Johnson was still too human-shaped to contain chaotic aethermorphic feedback. She took a picture and shook the salt off the quilt with a quick flick of the wrists.

The stop and start of his stream was petering off, and Martinez heard him start to rise. She looked at the last salting at the desk and bookshelf and gasped. The salt had formed an entirely different pattern, one she knew immediately—Furfur, Great Earl of Hell, currently bound hundreds of feet in the depths of the Salt Mine.

She pulled her equipment out of the bag and donned her gloves. Martinez picked up the offending bauble—a diminutive plushy green brontosaurus out of place with the other bric-a-brac on the bookshelf. When she made contact with the dinosaur, her amber pendant that fought off charms amongst other things grew warm on her chest. *I know you are not trying to target me!* she fumed as she put the tiny toy in a sack and surrounded it in salt. The warmth against her skin waned. She sealed it and stashed it in her leather bag just as Johnson flushed the toilet.

The water started running, and Martinez hastily took off her gloves and threw them in her bag. With a swipe of her hand, she knocked the salt off his desk. By the time he turned off the faucet and opened the bathroom door, Martinez was positioned outside it, waiting to assist him.

Johnson was started by her presence. "Who are you?" He suddenly looked very confused and fragile.

Martinez smiled. "Sam, I'm here visiting you. I'm Tiffany, Abby's daughter."

Johnson's friendly facade returned. "I have a sister named Abby," he affirmed.

"Why don't I help you back to your chair, Sam, and we can watch a little TV before I have to go back to work," Martinez spoke tenderly.

Johnson accepted her arm and cheerfully said, "I've never said no the company of a pretty girl."

Chapter Seventeen

Detroit, Michigan, USA
27th of September, 11:15 a.m. (GMT-4)

Martinez wove her muscle car in and out of traffic, shifting aggressively and punching her engine when she could. If it didn't mean she'd have to break the circle of his prison, she would've decked Furfur in his smug devil face. She took the exit to Zug Island, and the security guard at the entrance waved her through once she presented herself as Tessa Marvel of Discretion Minerals. Martinez pulled into the underground parking and backed her car in. She hoisted her bag on her shoulder and approached the elevators. Her charm had cooled once the plushy was secured, but it remained warmer than it normally was. She took that to mean there was some seriously bad mojo in the thing.

She flipped out the titanium key that granted access down to the first floor of the Salt Mine; all others could only go up. Abrams sat behind her clear ballistic glass window as always. When Martinez exited the elevators, the metallic slot in the wall opened and Abrams's voice came over the tinny speaker, "Please put your possessions in the slot."

Martinez deposited her bag inside. The metal door closed and the whirling sounds began as always. She heard a ding, but the door to the elevators beyond remained shut. "Angela, what's the deal?" she said a little surlier than she intended.

"Just a moment," she stalled with the impersonal courtesy found in service jobs. Finally, the doors opened.

Martinez walked straight into LaSalle, all six-foot-three and 230 pounds of him. She had contacted the Salt Mine before she left Evergreen Meadows to let them know what was coming, but she wasn't expecting to see him on entry.

He was holding her bag. "This way. Leader is waiting." He led her to the elevators she took to her fifth-floor office every day, but instead of pressing the button, he opened the locked door beside them. Martinez had never seen the door open before and often wondered where it went. It looked like today she was going to find out.

The hallway was narrow, with less than six inches clearance on either side of LaSalle's broad shoulders. The door shut behind her and she had nowhere to go but forward. The first thing she noticed was that her steps lacked the gritty traction of the salt floors found in most of the corridors. In this hallway, the floors were titanium and covered in glowing blue sigils.

She caught the more common ones—devils, demons, fae, shapeshifters—but there were others that were completely foreign to her. She didn't have time to analyze them because she had to hustle to keep pace with LaSalle's longer stride. Martinez deduced this was where people and things who failed security had to pass through—a magical gauntlet.

The hallway ended in a junction and LaSalle took a right

and opened the first door. "Please take a seat," he instructed, and allowed her to pass through the door first.

Like the floor of the hall, the small room was lined with titanium and covered in runes and wards. It was sparsely furnished—just a table and a few chairs. Martinez took a seat and inquired, "I thought you said Leader was waiting for me?" She rarely saw Leader outside of her fourth-floor office, much less this close to the surface.

Before Martinez could expect an answer, she was frozen in place and her mind just stopped. She could breathe, but that was about it. LaSalle unleashed his will and scanned her, each pass getting progressively deeper. She not only felt it in her bones, she felt it in her soul. Martinez didn't know how long she sat there, but she realized it was over when she could consciously blink. She had long suspected LaSalle was a practitioner, but this was the first time—to her knowledge—that she had been subjected to his magic.

LaSalle handed her a bottle of water and opened the door. Leader entered and approached the table where the contents of Martinez's bag were carefully laid out. Martinez had no recollection of LaSalle doing that. Leader was dressed in herringbone slacks, penny loafers, and a collared shirt under a cable-knit sweater—downright fancy for the otherwise casual attire. She put out her hand over the table and let it hover two inches above the array of items. Martinez opened the bottle of water and downed half of it in one go.

When Leader's hand came to the dinosaur from Johnson's

room, she stopped in her tracks. It was out of the salt and sack Martinez had transported it in. Martinez reached up to check if she still had her amber periapt on, and a wave of relief passed over her when she felt its familiar shape and contour under her fingertips. She felt no warmth emanating from it—whatever targeted her before couldn't in this room. Additionally, whatever LaSalle had done to her, the pendent had provided no protection. All she felt was the hawkish gaze of Leader as she turned around to face her. "Lancer, report."

Martinez drank more water and found she could speak again. "Last night, I verified Sarah Pullman's signature at her wake. While there, Meridiana made contact and requested a meeting with the promise of information about Sarah's death. When I went to 18 is 9 later that night, she claimed to have seen Sarah Pullman's final moments through her eyes and all signs indicated she was killed by an animator, but there was also a fiendish influence of unknown origin.

"I infiltrated the locked dementia ward this morning as a distant relative of Samuel Johnson. Upon investigation, I found three signatures: Johnson's on his person, a mixed signature where he was sleeping the night of Sarah Pullman's murder, and Furfur's signature on that toy. When I picked it up with my gloves on, it was actively trying to target me, but Weber's amber periapt gave me enough forewarning. I bagged it, packed it with salt, and called it in per protocol.

"Sarah Pullman's red jade donut is still missing. Chloe, Dot, and Weber agree that it is most likely the resistor Sarah

Pullman created as a detonator for her magical bomb. She was wearing it earlier the night she was killed. It wasn't on the body on discovery. It wasn't in her apartment. There was also no evidence of it at Samuel Johnson's. Detroit PD are also looking for it." Martinez didn't know what came over her, but it all came out in one coherent narrative and her inner critic was notable absent.

Leader paced the barren room. "In your opinion, do you think Johnson killed Sarah Pullman?"

Martinez nodded. "Yes, but I believe he was influenced to do so in his vulnerable state."

"Explain."

"I spent about an hour studying him and his mental landscape is convoluted, magically speaking. He went to the bathroom and forgot I was there and who I was. Yet, when I showed him a picture of Sarah Pullman, he remembered something from almost a week ago. It suggests that the part of his brain that casts and the memories associated with practicing magic are still intact, even though he can't remember other things in the short term. It would make him very susceptible to charming, and explain the mixed signature on the bed but his pure signature otherwise. Johnson isn't possessed by Furfur, but somehow, he's using him to perform magic."

"Like a puppet," Leader added thoughtfully.

"I also think there is another player," Martinez added.

One of Leader's eyebrows rose. "Continue."

"There is no way Samuel Johnson could have physically

taken the necklace from the crime scene. Someone ambulatory did. I also suspect the toy was placed in Johnson's room, perhaps by the same person but not necessarily."

Leader tilted her head ever so slightly. "What makes you say that?"

"Everything in the room except the hospital bed was from his life before he was diagnosed with dementia. The quilt on the bed, his desk, the books on his bookshelf, his framed photos—they all made sense, but the tiny green brontosaurus didn't fit."

A small smile almost formed on Leader's lips. "Who has access to Samuel Johnson?"

"Staff, allied health, nurses, doctors, and visitors to the dementia ward," Martinez answered.

"Find the necklace and any accomplices. Let's nip this in the bud."

"Yes, Leader."

All five feet of Leader strode out of the room, and Martinez went slack in her chair. She took a deep breath, and it felt like the first that was entirely her idea in a while. Whatever just happened, she was glad to be on the other side of it.

"Are you okay?" LaSalle came over and offered her another bottle of water.

Martinez waved it away. "I'm fine. I just feel like a rag doll that's been tossed around too much."

"It's part of the security protocol, to be certain you weren't compromised," he spoke earnestly. He sounded sincere, but she wasn't sure if it was an explanation or an apology. Martinez couldn't trust her perception so soon after her encounter with Leader.

"Can I pack the rest of my stuff up and go? I have work to do," she glossed over his statement. She had more important things to think about.

"Sure, I'll get you back to the elevators," he offered.

Martinez started putting things away while he watched. "I also need to go to the sixth floor. I'm going to need some supplies and expertise from the librarians."

"I can do that, too," he stated almost sheepishly.

Martinez hoisted her bag onto her shoulder. They walked in silence down the hall back to the main elevators. LaSalle presented his palm and retina before pressing the button to the sixth floor. Martinez noted his intent of riding all the way down, instead of getting off on the fourth floor before sending her on her way. The mechanics of the elevator were resounding in the quiet between them.

When the doors opened, Martinez stepped out immediately. LaSalle called out after her, "Drink lots of water and get something to eat. It helps."

Martinez kept her gaze forward. She could feel the salt crunch under her shoes as she walked. "In the future, warn a woman before you turn your full will on her."

"Who said that was my full will?" he replied just before the doors closed. She wondered about that as she made her way to the librarians. It reminded her that she really knew very little about the people she worked with.

Chapter Eighteen

Detroit, Michigan, USA
27th of September, 1:20 p.m. (GMT-4)

There was a strategy to summoning; it was more than just drawing the circle and sigils correctly. There was a vast array of supernatural beings, each with their own areas of expertise and price. It was about matching need with knowledge and weighing risk against gain. Practicing the arts was always a gamble, and summoning magical entities was no exception.

Martinez needed very specific information: who had taken Sarah Pullman's necklace from her and where it was now. Superficially, it seemed like a simple ask, but there were a lot of parameters to consider. It involved events that took place in the mortal ream. It sought knowledge of happenings in the near-past and the present. It involved a dead magician, a living magician who wasn't in complete mental faculty, and a devil.

She knew if Wilson was in her place, he would have gone devil every time, and the fiendish involvement was a pull, but ultimately, Martinez dismissed it for a couple of reasons. First, she had a deep distrust of them, even though intellectually she knew devils were bound to their word and always followed the letter of an agreement. The fact that they worked so hard to craft loopholes and corner cases to favor them in said agreement did not lessen her mistrust. Second, devils demanded blood payment. There were situations when it didn't have to be the caster's blood, but it was the preferred currency. Martinez didn't relish the thought of a devil having the taste of her blood in its mouth, even though she could theoretically use magic to scrub its memory of it after the fact.

Martinez had then considered fae. She wasn't bothered with their insistence on the summoner's veracity even though they never told the whole truth. It was basically like solving a riddle, and she was good at riddles. They had their peccadilloes and their temperament was both flighty and mercurial, but their price was generally less onerous than blood. Unfortunately, they weren't a good fit for the information required. If Martinez had needed to know something that happened on a different plane or something about fae, it would have been a no brainer.

She had contemplated summoning the ghost of Sarah Pullman, but there was no guarantee that her spirit hadn't crossed over into the Land of the Dead in peace. Not all people who died a violent death stuck around to haunt the mortal realm, and it was better to let sleeping dogs lie. If Sarah Pullman's spirit reached out to her, that would have been a different matter, but the last thing Martinez wanted was to start her on the path to becoming a poltergeist or worse.

Which left scrying. It was a technically a form of summoning in that the practitioner had to beckon the guides to reveal things. As Martinez understood it, the guides were not of the mortal realm, but they resided in some nebulous state that also overlapped the mortal realm. The guides didn't require a price per se, but that also gave them the right to refuse service. They only showed things to those they wanted to and weren't compelled to do more. While it was generally considered safe it was not without risk. Whenever a connection was made between the mortal realm and those not of it, it was a crapshoot. On paper, scrying was the way to go.

The problem was that historically, Martinez sucked at it. She had scried minor things to demonstrate she could do it, but it didn't suit her at all. She was willing to admit that some of it was prejudice on her part. All the trappings and woo-woo that came with popularization and commoditization drove her batty. Her fellow Salt Mine agent Aurora was the first magician skilled in scrying that didn't annoy the living hell out of her, and Martinez was pretty sure that was because her other specialty was blades.

But it wasn't only the insipid window dressing. At a gut level, Martinez simply didn't *get* the guides, and the ability to use magic came from a deep subtextual understanding. In short, what a practitioner could and couldn't do was keyed to that guttural comprehension. She parsed devils as esoteric lawyers literally from Hell. She appreciated that fae were basically the beautiful but cruel popular girls in high school who used cryptic speech for their amusement. But guides…who were they, what was their deal, and why did they voyeuristically watch humans do their thing?

Fortunately, Martinez wasn't a lone magician slogging through it on her own, and Chloe and Dot had some helpful suggestions. If Martinez was going to do this, she had to do it her way. There was no faking authenticity when it came to magic.

She had taken LaSalle's advice and stopped for lunch on her way back to Corktown. She'd called ahead to let Stigma know she was coming and bribed him out of the ritual room with promise of a bacon cheeseburger with fries. When he had gone into deep cover in the Russian Navy, he esoterically carried his gear on his skin, and over the past few weeks, he had been using the ritual room to systematically erase all traces of Boris Petrov from his skin, leaving it a blank canvas for whoever he was supposed to be next.

Martinez gathered her tools and she was pleased that there was nary a crystal ball or Ouija board. All she needed was her largest, deepest Pyrex dish, a bottle of water, the few strands of Sarah Pullman's hair obtained from the mortuary, half a cup of the baking soda used to absorb the booby trap on Pullman's journal, and—at the twins' insistence—scented candles. Apparently, the guides had a soft spot for tradition.

The basement was chilly despite having a vent, because it wasn't yet cold enough for the heater to kick on during the day. Martinez placed a space heater on either side of her before starting on the circle. She knelt on a gardening pad and placed her dish on the slate slab. She poured the clean water inside, filling it only halfway. With the chalk, she ringed it in a perfect circle and carefully marked each symbol, ensuring it contacted the curved circumference.

She unwrapped the candles—apple cider scented—and placed them around the circle. As she lit them with matches, the initial smell of singed wick was quickly overtaken by the spicy autumnal aroma. With the hair and baking soda on the ready, Martinez disrobed—the twins had suggested humbling herself to the guides to increase her chances of success, and it didn't get more humbling than naked and prostrate.

Martinez cleared her mind and let the scent take her back to a simpler time—an apple pie that just finished baking in the oven. She was anxious to eat it, but her mother told her it was too hot. Her grandmother gave her a bowl of green beans to snap; when they were all snapped, the pie would be cool enough to cut. Martinez grounded herself in that memory and that kitchen and let all the anger of the day slide away in that perfect moment.

Only then did she summon her will and begin her incantation. "To the guides that watch over us, a great wrong has been done. Someone has taken the life and work of one of us. I beseech you to show me who has stolen her power. Touch a piece of the fallen," she said as she dropped the hair into the water. "Taste her power," she requested as she sprinkled the baking soda in the dish.

Martinez closed her eyes and lowered herself to the ground. She began her litany, winding her will around the same words repeated over and over again. "Hear my plea."

Martinez's will and words saturated the mortal realm and seeped its way into the native home of the guides. They heard her application, no louder than the wind blowing through the trees, but persistent, like a hungry baby bird chirping for its mother. They did as they always do: they deliberated. Only if all three agreed would they intervene.

They had received requests from this one before, many of which were rejected in the past. It would have been easy to follow suit and cite precedent, but the eldest of them shushed their critique and bid her confederates to listen more closely; to see not just with their eyes and hear with not just their ears.

As they peered into the mortal realm, they perceived her openness of spirit. That was new. They saw her wounds, old and new, laid bare in supplication. They tested the edge of her righteous anger, focused and forged into hardened steel. They probed her heart and found her intent honorable and true. With one look to each other, they came to a decision. They stirred the waters and spoke, "Be still, sister, and see what you seek."

Martinez wasn't sure if the voice was inside her head or inside the room, but she heard it as clear as a bell. She opened her eyes and looked into the dish. The water roiled and as it stilled, a scene played out before her. It was Samuel Johnson's room, only he wasn't inside. The absence of the plush brontosaurus made her think it was sometime after her visit this morning. Her point of view was from the doorway, and a man walked through her to the desk. He opened a drawer and dropped a red jade donut inside before closing it again. She finally caught a glimpse of his face when he turned around to leave: Dr. Walker.

Martinez's heart was stirred by the vision, but she calmed herself before addressing the guides. "This man took an oath to first do no harm. Can you show me what possessed him to do something so heinous?"

The waters rippled and Samuel Johnson's room disappeared. The disembodied voice spoke again, "Some oaths supersede others." The waters stilled again to show the same man many years earlier. He was thinner in the middle and his hair was missing the gray of this morning. He was signing his name in a book: *Jeffery Thomas Walker*. "His fate is sealed, but there is still uncertainty in how all will come to pass. Not even we can know the whole of the future. Do what you must with this, sister."

Martinez bowed three times and praised them for their insight. As soon as she dismissed her will, she quickly dressed, blew out the candles, turned off the space heaters, and made it up the stairs without spilling any water. Stigma was just finishing his lunch and was two fries away from putting himself into a calorie coma. "It's all yours," Martinez announced as she poured the water down the sink. She grabbed her bag and keys. "Gotta go."

As her car warmed up, she sent off a message to LaSalle: *resistor located, on rte; Jeffery Thomas Walker, MD—devil's pact.* She reached into her bag and made sure she still had Tiffany Morale's work badge. She shifted into gear and headed toward Ann Arbor to retrieve Sarah Pullman's missing necklace.

Chapter Nineteen

Leader's desk was covered with all the files she had on Furfur, Great Earl of Hell, but currently, she was reading over Weber's numbers and Dot's projections. It would have taken the whole derby season to build enough power to reach the deepest level of the Salt Mine, but it was doable.

She had expected Furfur to *try* to escape, but she never thought he had the capability of something of this scale. How did he piece all this together from his confinement? She thought her wards had covered all contingencies, but apparently she was wrong. The pieces all fell into place when LaSalle had delivered Lancer's message.

Pacts with devils go back as long as there have been fiends and mortals, and the esoteric link created by pacts was very primitive but binding. The practice warranted its own entire administrative system in Hell, and Hell, being Hell, had turned it into a bureaucratic nightmare. It would have taken tremendous will and patience for Furfur to make a direct connection to a pact-human, not to mention the social taboo. It was simply beneath a devil of Furfur's stature to do anything more than wait out the clock and reap the souls in that numbers game.

Once she had that piece, she realized the single crack in the cage she'd put around the devil that Furfur had exploited. It was the only way of explaining what had happened. She cursed at herself for failing to think of it, but not too harshly. After all, she had to give credit where it was due. Routing an astral projection through the outer planes in order to contact a human in the mortal realm using the extremely tenuous connection of an old pact was ingenious and convoluted and nearly diametrically opposed to the social SOP of a powerful devil. More importantly, it didn't *technically* break any stipulations in his imprisonment agreement.

The instant Lancer had discovered Furfur's signature with her saltcaster, Leader had cut the power to his prison as a precaution, and it had proven wise. It stopped him from getting into any more mischief—no lights, no ability to use reflective surfaces to communicate through astral projection that wasn't *technically* astral projection as it was really outer planes projection. Now it was a matter of undoing what was already done and preventing such from happening in the future.

What Leader needed now was the particulars of this pact, and there was only one place she thought she could get reliable answers without drawing Hell's attention to the fact that she had a Great Earl of Hell bound in her basement. It meant phoning an old friend, one that she'd sort of lost touch with and should have called sooner but never seemed to find the time. Still, they had participated in more than one caper together over the years, and in a world where everyone else came and went, they still had each other, for better or worse.

She picked up the phone and requested an outside line. It rang three times before Meridiana picked up. "Hello?"

"Hey, Di," Leader's voice pitched higher than usual. "It's Penny. We have a problem. It's your dad."

Meridiana sighed. "Pen, please tell me you didn't lose him?"

"No, he's still here," she reassured the succubus, "but not as secure as I had originally planned. I'm calling because I need your help to lock down a loophole he's created."

Meridiana chuckled. Her caged father was like a toddler trying to escape a safety gate—relentless and resourceful. "He was always good at exploiting technicalities," she acknowledged. "What do you need?"

Leader sweetened her tone. "Can you find out the details of the pact he has with a Jeffery Thomas Walker?"

It was greeted with dead silence, and when the succubus finally spoke, she enunciated each word incredulously, "You want me to phone home and speak to the pact department?"

"I know," Leader acknowledged the gravity of her request. "But if I summon a devil and ask myself, there will be questions. It's not like your father is a nobody, or that I'm asking about an errant magician. But if you ask about your dad's affairs, it would raise less suspicion, especially considering your contentious history," she tactfully alluded to the past.

"I don't like it, Penny," Meridiana objected. "The last thing I need is for Hell to figure out I helped you trap him. My whole strategy was to lay low. The hair that sticks up is the one that gets cut."

"I don't think any devil would have a hard time believing your father was messing with you in the mortal realm using pact-humans. It sounds like the petty bullshit he would do for fun," Leader pointed out. "Plus, I have implicit faith in your creativity and charms."

Meridiana didn't speak for a few seconds, and Leader let her fume. She had made her argument and there was nothing to do but wait. Eventually, Meridiana begrudgingly agreed, "I'm not making any promises, but I'll see what I can dig up."

Leader breathed a little easier. "Thanks. Any chance you could do it sooner rather than later?" she pressed her luck. "I'm kinda trying to avert a disaster."

"Why is it that only call me with bad news or when you need something?" Meridiana inquired pointedly.

"Careful Di, you're dangerously close to sounding like your mom," Leader observed.

Meridiana's temper flared. "Penelope, you take that back or you can call Hell yourself!"

Leader held back her laughter and kept her voice level. "Mea Culpa. It's because I'm a shitty friend and a worse correspondent, and saving the world from itself is more than a full-time job."

Meridiana accepted her prickly apology—thorns and all—and answered it with understated sarcasm. "I'm just saying, if you called, I would pick up. Even if the world wasn't in grave peril."

"Noted," Leader said graciously.

"This doesn't have anything to do with your Agent Martinez and Sadie Pullman's death, does it?" Meridiana tested Leader after putting two and two together.

"And if it did?" Leader answered her question with a question.

"Second female magician around me to die within two months," Meridiana observed. "Makes me wonder if he already knows."

"Or he's so restrained that his exploit can only work locally in Detroit," Leader posited.

"Possibly," she mouthed despite the fact that she was less than convinced. "How's he doing it?"

"I'll tell you when I've got everything nailed shut again. But let's be realistic—you've toughed it out here for a millennia, while he's only been holed up less than three decades and whined about it the whole time. My money's on you. You've got the scrappy underdog thing going for you," Leader complimented her. "And unlike your father, you have friends. All he's got is a bunch of sycophantic devils who would backstab him in a heartbeat if they thought they could win."

Meridiana smiled. Penny always had a way with words. "Okay, I gotta go. Apparently, I have an important call to make."

"We'll talk soon," Leader promised and hung up.

Meridiana stared at her mobile and weighed whether she needed caffeine or alcohol for this endeavor. She went with both and liberally Irished her Americano. Even though she was banished from Hell, she was still the spawn of a Great Earl. She just needed to get her game face on.

She decided the best approach would be to go full devil, horns and all; this was no time to be subtle. Although the sky was overcast, Meridiana drew the curtains in her bedroom. She didn't want to have to explain to her neighbors why her Halloween costume looked so real. She put her mobile on vibrate and settled in with her drink.

As a succubus, she could adopt pretty much any combination of physical traits found in human variation, but when she transformed into her true form, it was always the same. Changing forms wasn't hard, but it was a process, especially transitioning from devil to human. There was a knack to comfortably tucking away the tail, wings, and horns, and getting it wrong was like having your underwear bunched funny under your clothes.

However, shedding the human form was fairly straightforward—once you perforated enough skin, the rest would tear like a paper towel off the roll. If she were being dramatic about it, she would make a small cut and let her wings burst out of her back and peel the skin back to exposure her horns. Nothing went to waste—her body absorbed most of the organic material to be used at a later time. It was a bit of a bloody mess by human standards, but fiends were hardly put off by some gore.

Meridiana laid out the plastic tarp she kept in her closet for just such occasions and gently shrugged off Leigh Meyer. Her leathery wings unfurled, and she flapped them a few times to circulate air around them. Her muscle memory kicked in as she whipped her tail a few times, slicing the air with a crisp snap.

She appraised her nude lithe form in the full-length mirror and decided to leave the viscera dangling just as it was. It was really quite becoming, like waking up to a good hair day for mortal women.

She summoned her will and made her connection to the Pact Department. It was one of those solidly good jobs for devils that were feisty enough not to be culled but not ambitious enough to get out of a desk job. Lucky for her, she had an older brother who worked in the filing department.

She was transferred three times, but eventually, she got her brother on the line. He was stunned by her appearance and it took him a moment to speak. "Meridiana? I haven't heard from you in ages!"

"It's good to see you too, brother," she greeted him warmly.

"How are things with the family?"

"Oh, you know how it is," he rolled his eyes, all four of them. "It's hard to keep track of who isn't talking to who and who is now in an alliance. I just keep my head down and show up when Mother calls me."

"You always were the sensible one, Azazel," she doted on him. "Perhaps I wouldn't be in my current circumstance if I had done the same. I should have known better to butt heads with our father."

"You seem to be doing all right," he said with a leer. "Still look as fresh as the day they pulled you out of the pit."

"Well, aren't you sweet," she remarked with a slight flitter of her wings. "But that's actually why I called. I think Dad's messing with me but I can't be sure. Do you think you could take a peek into a file for me?"

He shook his head condescendingly. "Meridiana, there's a formal request process: forms to be fill out, approval stamps to obtain—"

She threw her hands into the air. "That's all fine and well for devils in Hell, but how am I supposed to do all that from the mortal realm?" she asked rhetorically. "I just need you to look up *one* human for me. I think Dad has him pact-bound and he's using him to get at me."

"And why would Dad do that?" he questioned.

Meridiana tipped her horns and flicked her tail. "For the fun of torturing me."

Azazel nodded in comprehension. "Okay, just this once."

"Azazel, you're the best!" she emoted and fully whipped her tail. His eyes followed.

"Yeah, yeah, don't mention it," he mumbled before adding seriously, "to anyone."

"My lips are sealed," she stated and pantomimed for good measure.

He smiled, amused at the mortal ticks his younger sister had adopted. "What's the name?" he asked.

"Jeffery Thomas Walker," she answered.

He made noises while he searched. His files were meticulous, organized and cross-referenced four different ways. The file materialized in his hand in no time. "Well, he is one of Dad's…" His voice tapered off as he skimmed. "Hmm, that's odd."

"Found something?" she asked expectantly.

"You may not be completely crazy," he spoke as he pulled more files.

"Your confidence is overwhelming, brother."

He glared at her. "Do you want my help or not?"

Meridiana showed deference to him. "Sorry, please continue."

"What I was *trying* to tell you is that he has recently fulfilled his favors, all three in a short amount of time."

"How recently?" she asked.

"In mortal time?" Azazel did the math. "Within a fortnight."

Meridiana genuinely smiled—for all his faults, she did adore what an Anglophile he was. "Tell me more about this mortal."

He raised his gaze from the paper. "What are you going to do, Meridiana?" He knew his sister had a temper and the last thing he wanted was to go down for helping her.

"Relax. Dad won't find out, and last I checked, it was perfectly acceptable for fiends to toy with humans," she derided him. "Unfortunately, it can't be anything evil," she pouted, "but there's more than one way to skin a cat."

"Well, obviously," Azazel replied. "Moloch elucidated thirteen ways of degloving alone."

Meridiana rolled her eyes—*Nerd!* "Anyway, if you could just let me know everything in that file, I'll be out of your horns."

Azazel shook his head. *This is why I stay out of family business.*

*****

It was a small thing, no more than two centimeters across. It really did look like a miniature donut, only instead of deep-fried dough, it was a deep red jade. Weber felt a tiny spark on his fingertips when he made contact with the smooth polished surface. It could have been attributed to static electricity if he hadn't known better.

He had his directive: find a way to contain or control the

flow of magical energy before Detroit Roller Derby resumed practice in the drill hall. He didn't have much time, but he had to try. If he failed, the Salt Mine had no other option but to destroy Sarah Pullman's generator, and the thought of that broke his heart. It was elegant and innovative, an ideal blend of engineering and magic. He hated to confirm stereotypes, but on this occasion, he was willing to admit the German in him played a part—a well-made thing was of infinite beauty to him.

He sipped a cup of Oolong for contemplation. The easiest solution was to keep what Pullman had done but adapt it so it was no longer a bomb. The twins should have no problem attuning the jade, but the question was what to do with all that power and how to contain it safely.

He turned to modern power stations for inspiration, which constantly had to manage the influx of energy demand and supply. It boiled down to two basic strategies: store it as kinetic energy or potential energy.

When it came to electricity, the ubiquitous use of turbines in the generation of electricity made storing kinetic energy possible. It could be held in water through pumped hydroelectrical systems, in compressed air to be used when needed, or through the spinning motion of a rotor or flywheel. Sadly, magic wasn't powered by turning turbines, and such an infrastructure would take a lot of time and resources to create.

The other principle was to spend or convert that energy back into potential energy, which could then be turned back into kinetic energy when it was needed. In other words, a rechargeable magical battery. If he could divert the energy through the resistor into such a thing, it would store the magical potential until it was tapped. There would be some loss in the transfer between states, and they would have to be stored somewhere safe in case there was leakage, but it checked all the boxes. It siphoned the energy away from the drill hall before it reached dangerous levels, it stored the magical energy for later use, and it could be quickly and inexpensively implemented.

Unfortunately, magical batteries were a rarity. Even though battery technology was an old concept, magicians never took to it—why spend the karma to sink one's will into something with diminishing returns in the transfer? Weber finished his tea and selected a well-worn book from his shelves. He had three days to build a better battery, and there was nothing less than magical engineering perfection at risk.

Chapter Twenty

Jeff Walker followed the signs to I-94 West, tapping his thumbs on the steering wheel of his arctic gray BMW X5 M50i. Even though he was late heading home, he felt buoyant. Before he'd left Evergreen Meadows, he had called his wife and instructed her to stop whatever she was doing for dinner because he was taking her out, her choice.

Some women might have been suspicious at his gregarious mood—what did he do wrong and was this commensurate with the degree of the slip-up? But not Natalie. She simply put the marinating chicken back in the fridge and started going through her closet for something to wear. She was just thankful that the cloud of gloom lingering over him these past few weeks had lifted.

Walker switched off the news and opted for music. He stopped on classic rock, which was becoming more and more a euphemism for "the oldies" with each passing year. He caught the beginning of "Bohemian Rhapsody." He turned it up and started singing along.

It stirred up old memories, when his waist was trimmer

and his hair was longer, before he'd cleaned up and got out of Appalachian Ohio on a full scholarship. He was the first in his family to go to college and he'd leapt into unchartered waters headfirst.

What they hadn't told him about college was that tuition was just the tip of the iceberg. There were all the ancillary but related expenses: books, lab fees, school supplies, and clinical tools. He nearly choked on his own spittle when he found out how expensive textbooks were. Then there were the living expenses: housing, food, transportation, and healthcare. And, to top it off, there was the loss of income that came with going to school full-time. There weren't enough hours in the day to work forty hours a week and take a full course load, not that it had stopped him from trying.

Everyone had been so proud when he finished his undergraduate degree and was accepted into medical school. But after the excitement wore off, Walker had been left wondering how he was going to pay for all of it. Still, he'd preserved, applying for scholarships, fellowships, grants, and any other place that would give him money. For the rest, he'd taken out more loans. After all, he was going to be a doctor; everyone knew they made good money.

He'd breathed a sigh of relief when he made it to his residency—he was finally going to start getting paid for practicing medicine, albeit at a severely reduced rate for a doctor. He was pretty sure some of the nurses made more per hour than he did; not that they didn't deserve it, but he did go through eight years of college to get there. Why doctors didn't unionize like nurses was beyond him. Then, six months after graduation, the letters for loan repayment had started coming in. Adding additional stress to the situation, more often than not, he was giving money to his family to help them get by. They didn't understand residency, student loans, or accruing interest, just that he was a doctor now. He had money. Some of it was rightfully theirs. That's how things worked when you're poor.

Somewhere in his second year of residency, he had hit bottom. He was broke, depressed, and overworked. His girlfriend at the time had just broken up with him, because "I never see you and when I do, you're a zombie." He was doing a rotation at the Cleveland Clinic in winter, and the weather was as bleak as advertised.

One of the few free pleasures he had was availing himself to the university's libraries. Unlike the Cleveland Public Library, they were open all hours and he could visit in the middle of the night just after or before a shift. He had always taken solace in books. They represented endless possibility to him—all the things he could learn with just the turn of a page. When he felt the walls press in, a quick trip to the library always soothed him, surrounded by so many books.

The rift of Brian May's guitar broke his into morose memories as the bridge kicked into high gear. Walker started

177

singing again to lift his mood. After all, the trajectory of his entire life changed for the better that winter as well.

It was during one of those late night perusals. Walker was walking a familiar stretch of the stacks—old anatomy textbooks—when he found a book he had never seen before. It was old and leather-bound, with no name on the spine. Even stranger, it didn't have an assigned Dewey Decimal number. When he'd opened it up, it wasn't labeled as property of Case Western Reserve University. His curiosity had gotten the better of him, and as he flipped through the weathered pages, he'd caught the rough edge just so. Its sting was disproportionate for its damage—as paper cuts do—and a ribbon of blood emerged on his right index finger.

The taste of blood awakened something heretofore dormant, and a gaunt man with sallow, leathery skin and sunken eyes appeared behind Walker. Walker remembered him as being cachexic, even though his manner never seemed particularly frail. The man made him an offer—three wishes for three favors. All Walker had to do was sign his name in the book.

Walker was naturally suspicious—he had read the story of the monkey's paw. "What's the catch?" he'd asked.

"Your mortal soul will be forfeit upon your death," the man had replied stoically.

Walker didn't much abide by the religion beaten into him during his youth and focused on the logistics. "And you're not going to kill me to get my soul sooner?"

To this, the thin man spread his arms open with his palms up. "Things will unfold as they should."

Walker's analytical mind moved to the next point. "What about these favors?"

"Discrete tasks that could be asked of you at any time, and when the time comes, you will not refuse," the jaundiced man had said.

Such phrasing had compelled Walker to ask, "What happens if I refuse?"

"Something worse than if you had simply complied." The skeletal man then reached inside his pocket and produced three gold coins stamped with a horned figure, gleaming tauntingly in his hands. "This is a limited time offer, Mr. Walker. There is always someone willing to do the devil's bidding. Is anyone else offering you more?"

Pressed between eighty-hour workweeks of residency and the bills, Walker had signed and the emaciated man deposited the three coins in his hand. His bony hand had taken the book with him and vanished.

Walker had made his first wish on site: to have enough money to clear his school debt and practice whatever branch of medicine he wanted to. He had seen too many physicians pushed into specialties or surgery because the pay was too good, and his heart lay in general practice. In the blink of an eye, the first coin had disappeared from his hand and the remaining two went into his pocket.

Within a few days, he got a call—a previously unknown relative passed away and left him a sizable fortune. As far as Walker knew, there was no one in his family with money; otherwise his parents, uncles, aunts, siblings, and cousins would be hitting them up for money instead of him. He'd made good use of the windfall, paying down his debts and squirreling away the rest. He kept waiting for something bad to happen or to be asked to perform a favor, but it never came.

A few years after residency had ended, he decided to use the second coin after he met Natalie. She was everything he had ever wanted in a woman, and he'd wanted to secure a blessed life for them. And for many years, life was good. He had a job he loved, a family he adored, and most importantly, they had enough money. The gaunt man hadn't reappeared and no favors had been asked of him.

Over time, Walker had concocted a theory—if he didn't use the third wish, maybe the bill would never come. Like a good scientist, he'd locked the third and final coin away in his home safe and tested his theory. So much time had passed that he'd started to believe that he had hacked the system.

Then two weeks ago, while he was shaving, another face appeared to him in the mirror—the same horned figure stamped on his coins. Walker had nicked himself good that morning, and by the time he had stanched the bleeding with a tissue, the figure was gone. The good doctor had chalked it up to a figment of his imagination, but he could not dismiss it so easily when it appeared the next morning, and the next. Its piercing cerulean eyes followed him in the mirror with the grimmest of smiles.

Deep in his gut, he had known—his marker was being called. He had even considered trying to use the third coin to get out of the deal but didn't know what that would mean. Would he be shunted into an alternate reality where he was broke and didn't have Natalie? Would he be transported back to that winter in Cleveland? He didn't think he had it in him to live through those days again. Or worse, would the devil just take him for breach of contract?

After anguishing about it for a few days, Walker had made a decision. He had signed his name in the book under no illusions. His life had been blessed, and now it was time for him to live up to his end of the bargain. The first task was simple: take the toy left in his mailbox and leave it in Mr. Johnson's room at Evergreen Meadows. The second was bizarre but innocuous: be at a particular address under a certain window at a precise time to catch a falling necklace and pendant. When the face had appeared for a third time and told him to leave the necklace in Mr. Johnson's room, Walker had raised a query. He had not used his third coin yet—what did this mean? The blue-eyed face reassured him that this was the final task, and Walker would be asked to do no more once it was completed. As for his wish? That was free and clear once it was done.

Walker had been tempted to go immediately and be done with it, but decided to play it cool; breaks from routine were what got people caught. He had been startled when Mr. Johnson had company during his visit, but it was no matter. Visitors never stayed long, and it was simply a matter of slipping in afterwards while everyone was busy with lunch. He'd placed the necklace in one of the drawers and was gone.

Immediately, his heart had lightened. He could allow himself to dream about the future he and Natalie could wish for without fear of reprisal. The world was full of possibilities all over again.

An '80s power ballad followed Queen as he took the exit for Lima Township and drove through the back roads to his home in the country. No neighbors, a huge garden for Natalie, and once upon a time, plenty of room for the kids and all their 4H animals. As he pulled into the long driveway, he wondered where Natalie wanted to eat. Probably that French restaurant where the food was beautiful but the portions tiny, and they paired all your entrees with a different bottle of wine.

The sun was low on the horizon when he opened the door. The curtains were drawn but none of the lights were on. "Natalie, I'm home," he called out. "Sorry I'm late. I got called back to the hospital at the last minute and by the time I left, traffic was a bear," he apologized as he closed the door and put down his leather doctor's bag, the one his daughter had given him for his birthday a few years ago.

"Just give me ten minutes to change and I'm yours," he hollered as he went deeper into the house. His eyes had not yet adjusted to the relative dark and he stubbed his toe on entry to the living room. He cursed as he processed the pain and reached for the floor lamp switch. Before he made it, a bright beam blinded him.

Martinez emerged from a dark corner and tilted the light out of Walker's eyes just long enough for him to see her Glock pointing at him. "Take a seat, Dr. Walker," she instructed, motioning to the chair she had moved from the kitchen to the living room.

"Where's my wife?" he asked in a panic.

"Perfectly safe and sleeping in your bedroom," Martinez answered. "And she'll be fine as long you tell me the truth."

"Take whatever you want. Please, just don't hurt us," he begged and reached for his wallet.

"Ah!" Martinez tutted him. "Hands where I can see them, and sit down." She knew he was no magician, but that didn't excuse him from trying heroics. Things would be much tidier if she didn't have to shoot him.

He raised his hands high and sat in the high-backed maple chair. *Hail Mary, full of grace...* Martinez summoned her will and immobilized him. "You cannot move, but you can speak. Do you understand, Dr. Walker?"

He tested her words and found that he could not voluntarily move any of his limbs. "Yes," he replied, cowed.

"I'm here to give you a chance to explain your role in the death of Sarah Pullman," Martinez began.

"Who? Is that one of my patients? Look, I'm sorry if she's a relative of yours that passed, but this isn't the way," he tried to reason.

"Sarah Pullman was the previous owner of the red jade pendant you couriered to Samuel Johnson. She died Sunday evening."

Walker did the math and knew how it looked. "I swear I didn't have anything to do with it. I was just told to move it."

"And the dinosaur on Samuel Johnson's desk?" Martinez asked.

"Yes, that too," he backtracked. "But that's all I did. I put the stuffed animal in his room, I caught the necklace from a window, and I put it in Johnson's room." Walker tried to squirm but he couldn't make his body move.

"Do you understand that your actions have directly resulted in one person's death and materially harmed the well-being of someone in your care?"

"I didn't have a choice," Walker swore.

"You made your choice when you signed the book," Martinez proclaimed.

Walker ceased his efforts to move and suddenly wished to be very small and invisible. "How do you know about such things?"

"I'm here to tie up loose ends and neutralize threats,"

Martinez ignored his question and got to the gist of her visit. "If you can reassure me that you are neither, I can leave you be."

"I swear, it's all over." he whimpered.

"I'm afraid that's not going to be good enough," Martinez responded as she lowered the flashlight and secured her gun. Much to his surprise, that made Walker more concerned—he understood gunshot wounds but he had no idea what was coming next.

Martinez pulled a tea light candle from her pocket and lit it with a lighter. She slid the straight pin from its case and held Walker's limp right hand in her gloved hand. Even though the beam was no longer in his eyes, they were still adjusting, but he felt the prick of the needle he couldn't see. Still frozen in his seat, he could not even flinch.

She held pressure across the digit until a blob of blood formed on his index finger. With her other hand, she grabbed the candle and let the drop of blood drip into its flame. The resulting flare-up blazed like fat dripping onto a grill. Martinez released his hand and blew the candle out. "Now, I'm going to know if you make any more deals with the devil or cause any more mischief."

She put away her supplies and pulled out the shiny golden coin she'd liberated from his home safe earlier this afternoon. She held it in front of his eyes. "Additionally, I'm taking this. It will help mend the wrongs you have helped come to fruition."

"That's my wish. I earned it," he objected.

"Dr. Walker, those sound very much like the words of a loose end," Martinez cautioned him. "Consider this your third wish: you and your wife just survived this encounter."

Walker clammed up and Martinez spun her will into a different form. "Now, you are going to sit in the dark and stew on your mistakes for the next fifteen minutes. Then you are going to wake your wife with a kiss and take her out to dinner like you promised. Enjoy what is left of your life because your fate is sealed after your death, which will be considerably sooner if I have to return. Do you understand?"

Walker tried to shake his head but couldn't. "Yes, I understand."

"Good. And Mr. Walker? This never happened, and I was never here."

The sun had fully set when Walker blinked his eyes. He couldn't figure out why he was sitting in the dark on a dining room chair in the middle of the living room. He turned on the lamp and checked the time—no wonder he felt a little woozy, it was well past their normal dinnertime. *Just a touch of hypoglycemia*, he thought, and picked up a piece of candy from the dish.

He put the chair back in the kitchen and went into the bedroom. There were three dresses draped on his side of the bed with Natalie fast asleep on the other. She was still as beautiful to him as the day he first saw her. He leaned over and kissed her forehead. "Hello, sleepyhead," he greeted her.

Natalie smiled drowsily at his voice and stretched. "Oh, I must have dozed off. Is it too late for dinner?"

He sat on the bed and took her hand into his. "Sorry I was late—emergency at the hospital."

She opened her eyes and gave him a tender but knowing look. "I knew what I was signing up for…the lot of a doctor's wife. Should I just make some sandwiches?"

Walker shook his head. "I promised you dinner out, and that's what you're going to get. Put on your best dress, and we'll go into Chelsea for a nice meal. We'll be fashionably late, like the young people."

Chapter Twenty-One

Ann Arbor, Michigan, USA
28th of September, 9:35 a.m. (GMT-4)

"Mr. Johnson, calm down. I'm sure we can find whatever you're looking for if we look together," the young nurse aide's high-pitched voice squeaked despite her attempts at staying calm.

"Thieves! Stealing from an old man. Young lady, you should be ashamed!" Johnson yelled. Martinez entered the doorway just in time to see his raised hand.

Hail Mary… "Sam, what is going on?" Martinez laced her words with tranquility.

Johnson slapped his hand down on the armrest of his recliner instead of the aide. "They're taking my things," he said defensively.

"What things are missing?" she asked.

The bluster left him. "I don't remember, but I know I'm missing things."

Martinez nodded sympathetically and approached his recliner. "Why don't I stay and help you look while you have some breakfast? I brought you your favorite: apple fritter. I even have a hot coffee to go with it." She held out the sack and cup.

"Is it black?" he asked suspiciously.

"Of course," she answered. "Why don't we left this woman get back to work? There are residents that don't have any visitors that need her attention."

Johnson took the sack out of Martinez's hands and addressed the aide. "You could learn a thing from this young lady about how to treat your elders," he barked at her.

Martinez put his coffee on the movable stand beside him and both women waited until Johnson took the first bite of his donut. He seemed content and Martinez gave the woman a sympathetic look. "I think we're good. I'll push the call button if that changes." The aide nodded and left the room before things could go bad again.

He took a sip of the coffee and let out a satisfied hum. "The food isn't bad here, but the coffee is a different matter," he said to Martinez. "I'm not one to look a gift horse in the mouth, but who are you and what are you doing bringing me donuts?"

"I'm Tiffany, Abby's daughter. I visited you yesterday," Martinez answered patiently.

Johnson was smiling but his eyes were blank. "I have a sister named Abby," he said cheerfully.

"Yes, you do," she agreed. "I was wondering if we could talk some more."

He shrugged. "I've never said no to the company of a pretty

girl, especially one that brings me food."

Martinez closed the door and pulled up a chair. "We were looking at old pictures yesterday, and I was wondering if you would tell me about the past."

Johnson nodded. "What do you want to know?"

"What's your favorite memory? Something that always makes you smile when you think about it," Martinez proposed and started spinning her will.

"Our perfect day," he said fondly. "That's what Julie called it. We were just married—rich in love but stone broke. It was a Sunday, and we didn't have to work. We slept in and made love. We had pancakes afterwards and spent the afternoon at the lake. It was summer and sunny," he added.

"What was she wearing?" Martinez prompted him, laying down the first layers of her will around him.

"Her blue dress with the little white flowers, and a white sweater. That woman could catch a chill at high noon in the Sahara. And she had a wide-brimmed hat to keep the sun out of her eyes. She had the prettiest eyes. Cornflower blue. And she had her hair tied back with a white ribbon." He had a far-off look in his eyes. If he thought hard enough, he could see her now in his mind's eye. He'd forgotten many things, but not her face. Never her face.

Martinez continued threading her will and elicited more details. "What did you do at the lake?"

"What young lovers do on a lazy Sunday. We soaked in

the sun, walked along the shore, talked about everything and nothing. We had all the time in the world back then. I remember she wanted ice cream. Her favorite was chocolate, but she was afraid of spilling it on her clothes. I told her life's too short to eat vanilla when you want chocolate, and I'd buy her a new dress if that happened." His eyes turned rheumy at the thought.

"Did she end up getting chocolate?"

"She did. Ate every last drop without spilling. I think she was extra careful, because she knew I meant what I said and didn't want me to spend our money on new dresses. Julie was like that," he chuckled. His mind was somewhere else entirely, some place happy and unaware of all he had lost and had left to lose. Martinez had done her homework; he had a do not resuscitate on file—no heroic measures. There wouldn't be any CPR, feeding tubes, or intubations.

She was nearly finished with the crystalline ball of will that encased him. She leaned in and touched his hand. "Sam, you're getting tired. I want you to go to sleep and live in that memory forever."

He turned to her and grinned. "Good night, young lady."

Martinez watched him close his eyes. "Good night, Sam."

As soon as he was asleep, she took out her hag stone and made one last sweep to make sure she hadn't missed anything. Then, she stowed his copy of *Sacred Geometry* in her bag. Before she left, Martinez draped a blanket over his reposed body and slipped out the door quietly, even though there was no risk of waking him.

Martinez drove back to Corktown in silence. Every second, the world pressed down harder. Her murder victim was actually a bomb maker. Her killer was also a victim, just an old man who *couldn't* know what he was doing. His puppet master was out-of-bounds because he was already imprisoned, and his accomplice was just some putz whose biggest mistake was having a moment of despair and weakness in his twenties. After she closed her front door behind her, she took a second to lean against the thick piece of steel. It was bullet resistant and warded as all get out, but right now, its most appealing feature was that it was holding her up.

"Is that you, Teresa?" Stigma called out from the kitchen with a ball of his will ready in case it wasn't.

"Yeah," she hollered.

"Do you have a preference for dinner?" She heard the rhythmic click of his crutches. "We can have chicken or pork loin." When he reached the entryway, he saw all was not right. "You look like you've been put through the wringer. You all right?"

She dropped her bag and smiled weakly. "Just a little tired, but I finished my case."

Stigma steered her to the couch with his crutches. "You're so wrecked you can't even lie convincingly. Take a load off and I'll be back with tea."

"With your crutches?" she objected.

"I'll manage. You—couch," he ordered. To his surprise, she compiled.

He swung into the kitchen and started the water. He loaded a mug with chamomile and lavender and reached the top shelf where she hid the cookies she wasn't supposed to have—out of sight, out of mind; break in case of emergencies.

Martinez watched Stigma bring out supplies one at a time, single-crutching it to have a free hand to carry things, the last being a hot cup of tea. "Thanks," she said as she warmed her hand on the mug and turned the honey bear upside down. The thick stream of golden liquid oozed into her cup.

He retrieved his other crutch from the kitchen and found her eating cookies and drinking upon his return. He took a seat on the other end of the couch. "You wanna talk about it?" he asked.

"Not particularly," she answered as she sipped her tea and took another cookie from the package.

Stigma had been there before; some things couldn't be fixed—broken once could mean broken forever. She would just have to take the pieces and build whatever she could out of them. But first, she had to clear the rubble. He considered all that he'd ascertained from his time under her roof and hospitality and came up with a better proposal.

"You wanna lean against me and watch TV while I pretend not to notice that you're crying?" he offered.

Martinez wobbled her head and set her mug down. He grabbed the remote and settled himself for official pillow duty. He turned on Real Housewives of somewhere, then outstretched his arm and she put her head on his chest. Her breathing became shallow and erratic as she started sobbing. He turned up the volume and put his hand on her shoulder. He gently rubbed up and down until the shaking stopped.

Chapter Twenty-Two

Detroit, Michigan, USA
28th of September, 4:30 p.m. (GMT-4)

Leader rode the elevator down to the sixth floor and walked through the crystalline halls until she reach another elevator—this one venturing deeper into the earth. She pressed the button for the twelfth floor, the lowest level that housed only one thing: Furfur, Great Earl of Hell.

When the elevator doors opened, she took out her flashlight and found her way to the breaker box on the wall. The room flooded with light, and Furfur stopped mid-pace to greet his visitor.

"Am I done with my time out?" he precociously asked.

Leader stared him down with her cold gray eyes. "That depends. Are you ready to be good?"

He made a flippant gesture. "I'm always good."

Leader chided him, "You've been busy, Furfur. Why can't you just behave?"

"Why can't I flay your skin and devour your soul?" he rhetorically answered. "Wasn't it a human that said you can't always get what you want, but if you try sometimes, you get what you need?"

Leader sighed. "You leave me no choice, Furfur." She pulled out the golden coin bearing his likeness. His smarmy facade became very serious. He instantly knew what it was. It was his coin, *the one free and clear coin.* "I wish that you will not try to shorten the duration of our agreement." As soon as she uttered the words, the coin disappeared. Furfur had a sickened look on his face.

"You and I are going the distance, Furfur," Leader stated as fact. "Maybe in time, you can win back some of your privileges with some good behavior. Until then…" Leader went to the switch and killed the electricity again.

The litany of curses he flung at her bridged many languages. Most of them were common enough, but she made note of obscure ones she recognized. It wasn't often the devil let anything slip about himself. She paused at the elevator, switched off her light, and waited.

She had her reservations about Meridiana's plan, despite the succubus's reassurances that the original agreement had been between Walker and Furfur. The coins were registered to Dr. Walker at their issuance, and as such, Leader's use would come up as Walker using his final coin. The wording of the wish simply sounded like a man trying to make sure the devil didn't cut his life prematurely short, now that he had performed all three favors. Still, Leader had doubled-checked herself to make sure that using the coin would not constitute a de facto pact with her. The only devil she would even consider doing a favor for was Meridiana, and it wouldn't be through litigious compulsion.

Leader stood in the dark, listening to Furfur unravel, and savoring the irony. In his desperation, he had left himself wide open. He was now bound by his own power to not work against her, at least not in any fashion that would hasten his release from imprisonment. Now that he was on both ends of the bargain, he had no more wiggle room. There couldn't be a loophole as it was him binding himself. That brand of comeuppance reminded her of the old days; it was almost oracular. As soon as she was satisfied that his rage was genuine and not just an act, she summoned the elevator and ascended.

Chapter Twenty-Three

Detroit, Michigan, USA
29st of September, 6:05 p.m. (GMT-4)

David LaSalle pulled up to the two-story colonial and saw the black Hellcat parked in the driveway. He grabbed the package from the passenger seat and approached the front door, wary of the wards—Fulcrum was no slouch when it came to security. When he rang the doorbell, the eight-note chime of Westminster cut through the background music. He tapped his fingers to the beat while he waited.

Martinez shushed Stigma and turned down the volume of the music before checking the window. She was surprised to find LaSalle on her doorstep. She grabbed her phone—did she miss his call? She straightened her clothes and ran her fingers through her hair. A wave of warmth and the smell of roast pork rolled over him when she opened the door.

"Hey! What are you doing in my neck of the woods?" she greeted him casually.

The smell of fresh baked bread wafted in his nostrils, but LaSalle kept on task. "Just here to drop off a package for your houseguest."

"He's in the kitchen cooking. You're more than welcome to come in and give it to him yourself." She opened the door wide. LaSalle took a millisecond to brace himself, and he stepped across the threshold. Nothing happened. "Well, in or out, mister. You're letting all the heat out," Martinez repeated the well-heard rebuke of her childhood home.

She closed the door behind him and called out, "You have company."

"Is it Alicia? Or maybe Joan?" Stigma guessed. "LaSalle!" Stigma exclaimed when they entered the kitchen. He and Martinez exchanged a look as she passed him for her glass of wine. "What a pleasant surprise. Did you miss me?"

LaSalle gave him a smirk. "I'm here to give you your new identity. I thought you would want to get your hands on it as soon as it was ready, so I offered to drop it off on my way home."

Martinez sipped her wine—*LaSalle gets time off and has a home outside of the Salt Mine?*

"Seriously?!" Stigma gasped in disbelief as he put down the spatula. He took possession of the package and tore into it like a kid at Christmas. It was all in there: driver's license, US passport, loaded bank accounts, credit cards—everything an adult needed to function in the US. In time, the international things would fall into place, but there was a light at the end of the tunnel for Stigma. He was one step closer to returning to the field. He scanned the documents for a name, and his face froze.

Martinez read his expression. "It can't be that bad...they gave me Tessa Marvel. I should be a superhero in spandex and a cape with that name."

Stigma looked at LaSalle. "This has to be a joke."

"I swear I didn't pick it. Maybe you pissed off someone in records," LaSalle suggested.

"Well, now you have to tell me!" Martinez was bursting at the seams.

LaSalle's lips twitched as he fought off a grin. "Say hello to Aaron Haddock," he unveiled Stigma's new cover.

Martinez lost it and she laughed with her whole body. She had problems breathing, and tears came to her eyes. When she snorted, LaSalle could no longer contain his amusement. He had been sitting on this one the whole ride over.

"Har, har, laugh it up. Stick a guy in the Russian Navy and give him a fish name when you pull him out," the newly christened Haddock commented.

When Martinez regained her ability to speak, she apologized, "I'm so sorry for you, but this is exactly what I needed. If it makes you feel any better, I'll can call you A-A-Ron," she offered. Stigma snickered.

"A-A-Ron?" LaSalle asked, confused.

"Key & Peele. They have these sketches where the substitute teacher from the inner city pronounces the white kids' names wrong," Stigma answered him while Martinez wiped her tears away.

"Be-loc-ke? De-nice?" Martinez tried.

"Is this from a show?" LaSalle guessed. "I don't really watch much TV."

Martinez and Stigma threw their hands up and immediately began to conspire. "I'll get drinks, you line up the clips," Martinez suggested.

"Grab me a beer? Roast should be done in thirty minutes," Stigma noted.

"What's going on?" LaSalle asked.

Stigma picked up his crutches and guided him to the laptop in the living room. "The miseducation of David LaSalle," he replied. "You probably don't get that reference, either," he ribbed him.

"Take it easy on him. Leader keeps him on a short leash," Martinez teased. "What do you want to drink, David?" Martinez asked him.

He was unaccustomed to hearing someone other than Leader call him by his first name. It was nice. "I'll have whatever you're having," he replied.

"Red wine from a box it is," she proclaimed as she dispensed it. There was a playfulness in her demeanor that he only got glimpses of at work. She handed him a full glass. "Get ready to laugh your ass off."

LaSalle fell down the rabbit hole of internet videos with Stigma while Martinez kept topping off his drink. In the process, he had taken his jacket off, and before he knew it, there was a call that dinner was ready. LaSalle was about to make his excuses when he saw the spread Martinez had laid out: a tossed salad, roasted potatoes, carrots, and beets, a basket of warm rolls, and a golden log on a platter. There was already a place set for him.

"Is that Beef Wellington?" LaSalle asked is awe.

"Close. Marinated pork loin wrapped in Filo," Stigma answered. "I made it," he said with a gleam in his eyes. LaSalle looked dubious.

"Don't worry, I supervised him," Martinez reassured him. "But the trifle in the fridge is all him."

"Do you guys always eat like this?" LaSalle asked as he took his seat. Platters and plates were passed around.

"No, but it's Sunday night dinner," Martinez answered nonchalantly, "and all the leftovers become lunch for the week ahead." She passed him a plate with a slice of pork loin encased in flaky pastry. "Now tell me what you have learned from the internet."

While they ate, they talked about all manner of unimportant things with gusto, and LaSalle joined in when he could. He observed Martinez and Stigma, the rhythm of their patter and how one would nod in comprehension before the other had finished their sentence. He counted the number of times she touched Stigma's arm or hand: six. It would be fair to say they got along well, and he wasn't sure how he felt about that.

One thing they didn't talk about was work. There were allusions to "that time I was in X for work" but the anecdote afterward had nothing to do with magicians, monsters, or securing disruptive items. For those ninety minutes, they were just three people having dinner and drinking a little too much.

"The trifle is very good," LaSalle complimented Stigma.

"Thank you," he tipped his glass in recognition. He turned to his housemate, "Is it okay with you if I skip the movie tonight? I want to spend some time figuring out the new guy."

"Sure," Martinez said breezily. "No worries, I'll clean up."

"In that case, I bid you guys a good night. I'm going upstairs to figure out how to make Aaron Haddock a bad mother—"

"Shut your mouth!" LaSalle hit his mark.

Martinez grinned. "You are never going to be as cool as Shaft, Haddock."

"Just wait until I figure out my ink. Mild-manner mining engineer advisor at Discretion Minerals by day, man of mystery at night," Stigma quipped. "Thanks for bringing this by tonight, LaSalle."

"No problem, Haddock." He chuckled at the name again before turning to Martinez. "You need help with the dishes?"

"I won't say no if you're offering," she replied as she rose from the table. She packed up the leftovers while LaSalle brought the plates to the counter, scraped the food off, and systematically stacked them for washing.

"You and Aaron seem to be getting along well," he made

conversation.

"I kinda had to make it work," she pointed out after she stashed the last piece of Tupperware in the fridge. "When you dropped him off on my doorstep, I didn't really have an idea of how long he'd be staying." She rolled back her sleeves and plugged one side of the sink before filling it with hot soapy water.

"You think he's staying after the cast comes off?" he asked.

She started with the glasses before scrubbing the dishes. "God, I hope not," Martinez confessed. "There are parts of cohabitation that are nice, but it's also exhausting to come home and consider someone else's needs every night." Martinez caught the look of relief on his face in her periphery. "But I've had worse roommates, and I'm more than happy to have him until he gets on his feet. It will take time to find a place, even after he gets the cast off."

He rinsed the soap off the dishes and placed each piece for drying. "Where are the kitchen towels?" he asked.

"On your right, second drawer down," she answered. She watched him sideways as he methodically dried one piece before moving to the next. "So how does Leader cope when you are off? I'm pretty sure shit goes down twenty-four seven around the globe."

"I'm not her only assistant, just her favorite," he replied. "What we do is important, and making her life easier makes everything go easier."

"Happy mommy, happy family," Martinez aphorized. "Except she's hardly maternal. More like a stern matriarchal elephant," she mused. "Don't tell Leader I call her a pachyderm," she ordered him. "That's the wine in the box talking."

He laughed. "Never happened," he reassured her. They worked in sync, passing glasses, plates, platters, and utensils down the line until all were clean, dry, and put away.

Martinez put the kitchen to bed and walked him to the entryway. "Thanks for helping. You wanna stay and watch a movie?" she offered. "Aaron and I were going to watch thirty-one days of scary movies in October, but we couldn't cull the list down to just thirty-one, so we started early."

LaSalle hesitated. "I should probably get going."

Martinez screwed her face up.

"What?" he asked defensively.

"I'm trying to decide if that's an 'I don't really want to stay but can't think of a better way to leave' or 'I want to stay but I'm not sure it's a good idea.'"

"Does it matter if they both lead to the same ending?" LaSalle questioned philosophically.

Martinez took a half step toward him and brushed aside her bangs. Her eyes were fuzzy from the wine but purposeful nonetheless. "An insightful man recently told me life is too short to pick vanilla when you want chocolate just because you're afraid it might make a mess of your clothes," Martinez confided to him in an intimate tone.

She was close enough that he could smell her shampoo, and his voice dropped nearly an octave. "What do *you* want?" he asked.

Martinez gave him an effortless grin. "I wouldn't have invited you to stay if that's not what I wanted, but to answer your question, I'd like you to do what you want to do, provided you know what that is."

LaSalle wasn't sure how to reply and stood still and silent.

"I'll make it easy for you. I'm going to sit on the couch and watch *The Shining*—the Jack Nicholson one. You're either going to join me or leave. Either way, I'm good." Martinez theatrically showed her hands like a blackjack dealer leaving the table and slid out of the conversation before it became any more painfully awkward.

She started setting up the television with the cluster of remotes. Once the movie was queued up, she turned down the lights in the living room—scary movies were meant to be seen in the dark. "Got room on the couch for one more?" LaSalle asked from behind.

Martinez moved from the middle to one side. "Maybe, but it's a love seat. We may have to smoosh to fit."

Epilogue

Detroit, Michigan, USA
2nd of October, 7:15 p.m. (GMT-4)

"Lessie, protect your jammer!" Coach Kent yelled as the pack skated by. The voice echoed in the high ceiling of the newly renovated drill hall against the backdrop of wheels in motion against the track. She had the Motor City Rollers divided into two teams to jam and they were battling it out in fine form. "ValKillrie, don't let her back in—back block!"

She put her whistle to her mouth and gave a short blow. "Mantis, foul! Come on, ladies, you know the rules. Bend them, don't break them." Scarlet took a whip off Lessie's shoulder and broke through the pack. "That's what I like to see!" Kent hooted with a smile. It was good to be home, even if this was the last season here.

Amidst the noise, she didn't hear the door open and close behind her, but the hair on the back of her neck stood up as she perceived someone approach. "Tracy Kent," a clear, crisp woman's voice said her name. It wasn't a question, but a statement.

She didn't look up from the track. "I'm her, but I'm a little busy at the moment," Kent brushed the woman off, but she was not deterred.

"I'm here to discuss Detroit Roller Derby's future at the drill hall, and I understand you are on the council that makes such decisions," she said persistently.

Kent glanced at the speaker—a diminutive woman with salt-and-pepper hair dressed in a suit. She was barely five feet tall but she didn't seem cowed by Kent's imposing stature or gruff demeanor. Perhaps it was the wall of muscle standing behind her. Although he too was wearing a suit, Kent guessed his secretarial skills weren't what got him the job.

Kent blew three short whistles and clapped the same number of times. "Good jam, ladies. Take five, get some water, and run some drills," she directed the team. Kent turned her attention to the bizarre pair behind her. "You have five minutes."

Leader smiled. She liked a woman that didn't have time for nonsense. "I would like you to present this to the council at their next meeting," she said simply as LaSalle produced a large sealed envelope. "It contains a rental agreement between the Masonic Temple and Detroit Roller Derby for the drill hall for next season with a clause for automatic renewal. There is also paperwork setting up the Sarah Pullman Memorial Foundation to finance the operation and organization of the Detroit Roller Derby, as well as a check for the initial funding. All the council needs to do is sign the paperwork and file it."

Kent took the folder and flipped through the pages. Her eyes bulged when she saw the new rental rate, but not as much as when she saw the amount of the check, written from Discretion Minerals. After the shock waned, her suspicions flared. "The Detroit Roller Derby isn't for sale, directly or indirectly. What's your game?"

The coach's thinly veiled accusations rolled off Leader. "We don't want to interfere with the running of the league, we just want to make sure you have a place to jam," she reassured her, cherry picking Kent's own lingo.

"You expect me to believe some company wants to give us this money for nothing?" Kent asked incredulously.

"There is a stipulation that the Detroit Roller Derby can only access the Foundation's funds if they are housed in the drill hall. Ms. Pullman felt strongly about the drill hall being its home and this arrangement honors that wish," Leader answered.

"That's it? We just have to stay at the drill hall?" Kent restated for clarity.

"Feel free to have your lawyers look over the legalese, but I assure you, it's all above board," Leader replied. "I think it would be in good taste to retire Slashy Sadie's number and put up a commemorate plaque of some sort. Perhaps some season tickets, but that isn't an explicit requirement," Leader deadpanned.

Kent shook her head and grinned. "Lady, for this much money, you can have all the season tickets you want."

LaSalle handed Kent a business card while Leader wrapped

things up. "This is the number for the department than handles our corporate philanthropy. Call if you have any further questions or need additional guidance on how to proceed."

Leader and LaSalle were about to leave when Kent halted them. "Wait, I didn't get your name."

Leader extended her hand to the robust woman in front of her. "My apologies. Angelica Zervo, CEO of Discretion Minerals."

Kent took a good look into her steel gray eyes and saw something kindred in the petite woman—hard, resolute, unyielding. "Thank you for doing this, Ms. Zervo."

Leader gave a rare smile. "Be sure to send those tickets, Ms. Kent. I look forward to an exciting season."

As Leader walked to the door with LaSalle close behind her, she heard the shrill of Kent's whistle, hustling her team back to order. As they walked back to the car, Leader commented, "That went well."

LaSalle knew from experience that she wasn't expecting a reply, and he merely nodded and opened the car door for her. Leader glided into the back seat of the heavily tinted black SUV. It was bullet resistant, bomb proof, and magically warded. It was also extremely comfortable, with heated leather seats in the back.

Her phone buzzed in her pocket, and she pulled it out while LaSalle got behind the wheel and warmed up the engine. She tapped on the new email and raised her brow when she saw the sender's name: Wilson, David.

Leader, if you have received this email, it means I have not returned in a lunar month and am probably dead, it started.

"Where to next?" LaSalle asked.

"David, please take me back to the office," she politely requested before returning to the screen and scrolling down.

THE END

The agents of The Salt Mine will return in *Rest Assured*

Printed in Great Britain
by Amazon